EYE CONTACT

SELENE dePACKH

TREPIDATIO
PUBLISHING

ISBN: 978-1-68510-166-4 (trade paper)
ISBN: 978-1-68510-167-1 (ebook)
Library of Congress Catalog Number: 2026931948

First printing edition: January 30, 2026
Published by Trepidatio Publishing in the United States of America.
Cover Design and Layout: Selene dePackh
Interior Illustrations: The Public Domain Review (*Early Illustrations of the Nervous System by Camillo Golgi and Santiago Ramon y Cajal*)
Edited by Sean Leonard
Proofreading and Interior Layout by Scarlett R. Algee

Trepidatio Publishing, an imprint of JournalStone
1400 North Wood Rd.
Murphysboro, IL 62966

Trepidatio books may be ordered through booksellers or by contacting:
JournalStone | www.journalstone.com

As always, for Suzanne, who came out on the raw end of the "in sickness and in health" deal. If, as Ram Dass says, we are all just walking each other home, she has carried me a good share of the way.

CONTENTS

EYE CONTACT

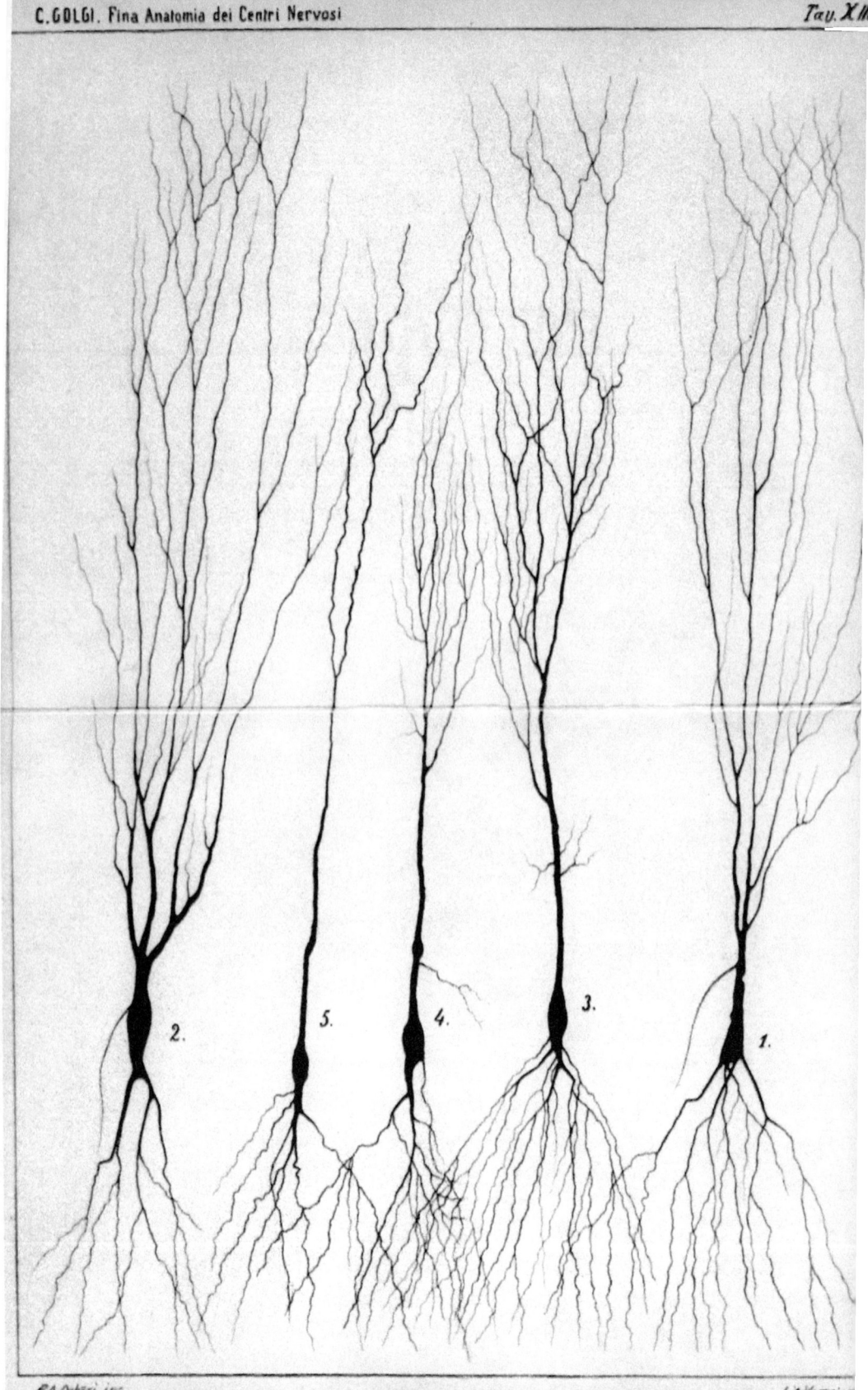

PLEASED TO MEET YOU

My name is Rowena, Ro for short. I had two friends when I was nine, although it's hard to say how long ago that was. Years have a different meaning where I am now. Sometimes I still see Sybille and Miles, but it gets harder to find them as they search for their own ways through. I think, or maybe hope, Sybille will probably get out of here before I do if she makes up her mind to, but Miles may have to stay longer than me. He was the one who hung himself. Sybille didn't want to come here; it got forced on her, and she fought it until she gave out. Me, I knew it was casting a line to reel me in, and I failed to get out of the way of the hook, you could say.

I tried to show Sybille a few things I knew about this place before she died. I could feel it coming for her, and I wanted to give her whatever I could to help her pass through. She'd be free now if she weren't still grieving for the child she died from. She was never going to live through that pregnancy. I'd be inclined to say she knew that, but she refused to believe it. She was almost eighteen, but her body wasn't cut out for carrying another life. It was barely holding together trying to carry hers.

That pure-hearted optimism is why I treasure her, and also why she makes me want to throw myself into the Void sometimes. The Abyss is the very center of this Infinite Sphere whose circumference is nowhere, and, trust me, if you look into it, you don't want it noticing you. That's the only quick way out, and the exit is permanent if it accepts your offer. Once most of our denizens get a good sense of it, they re-think any love they had for its embrace. It usually shows its mercy by spitting back out the only ones who really want it anyway, with time penalties added to their sentences. It loves indifference and hungers for the emptinesses outside itself that it doesn't already have.

Sybille isn't going to find her baby, poor angel. It was too early in its development to have formed any attachments, even to her. Just a palm-full of soft, watery, misshapen proto-lizard. Developed enough to kill her when its growth demanded more than she could give though. Her sister tried to get her to abort the thing before it was too late, and refusing that was the crime that landed her here.

The way you get punished for throwing your life in the garbage disposal is that you learn what you could have been. You don't get to avoid the work. I'm an old linguistics professor, with white hair and tenured attitude, except I froze to death when I was a kid, trying to run away...run away from a lot of things. I suppose I'll have to get around to telling you about that at some point.

Not everyone stuck here is the guilty party, and I shouldn't pretend to know more about Sybille's situation than I do. The particular interdimensional acreage I'm fettered to is layered with wounded souls, mostly kids, who endured things ghastly enough that the Abyss sometimes accepts them into its obliterating compassion.

Here are some stories about my friends and adversaries, some of them on this side and some still out there for the time being. Sometimes it's me telling them and sometimes it isn't. I'm not sure how they turn out, so I might be fooling myself about having any say in it at all.

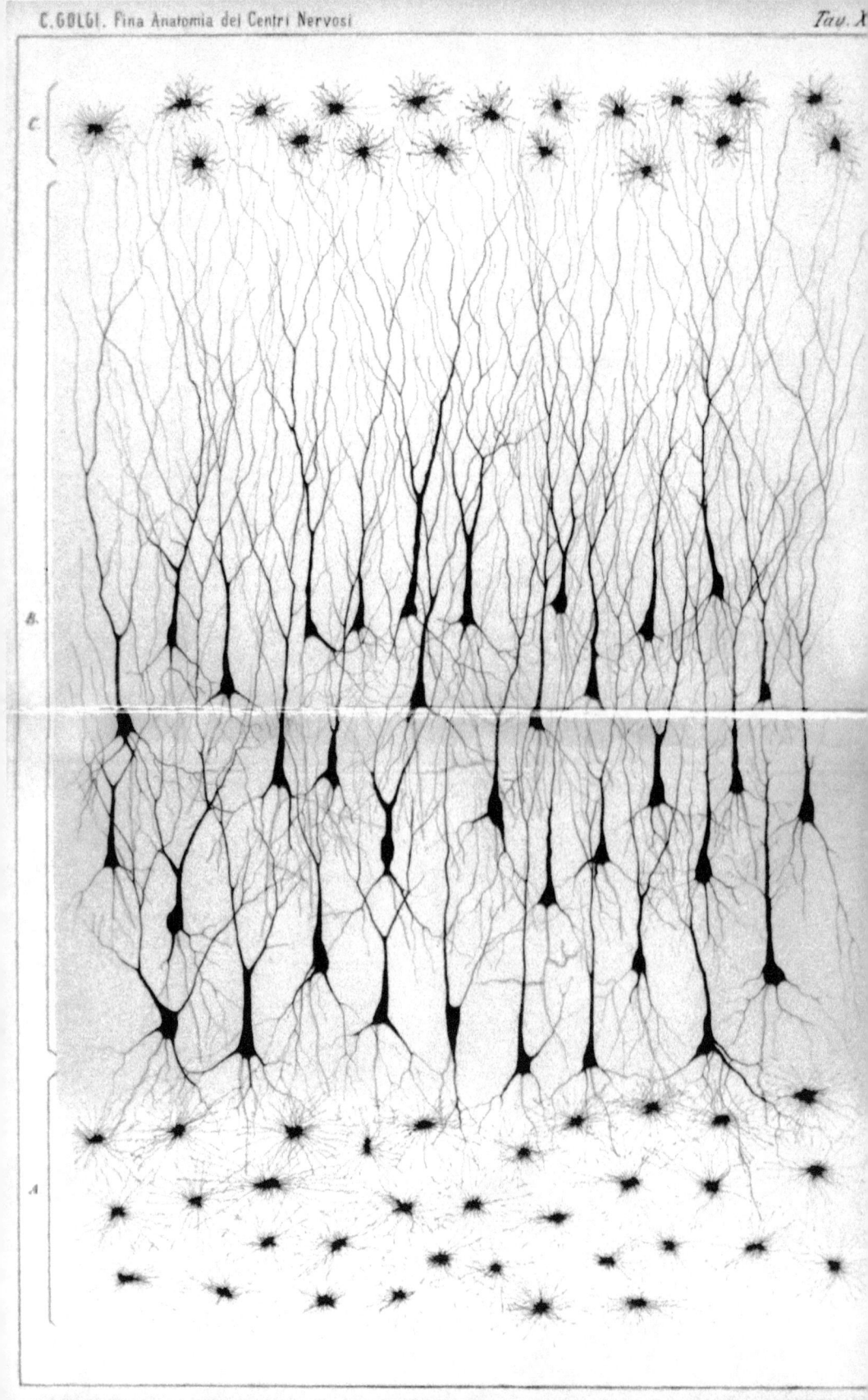

PASSED PAWN

A large shadow slipped along the treeline, then merged into the deeper gloom of the woods. The smooth slink of its movement had a syncopation to it, like an animal with an injured foot. Brian's glance flicked after it as he willed his body to stay motionless in his chair, facing the heavy desk in front of him. His mind kept returning to the dark shape, too big for a native predator, but too low-slung for a whitetail. He could almost imagine the thing was holding something limp in its mouth, but he knew his eyes weren't sharp enough to see that level of detail from where he sat. He told himself it must have been reflections within the multi-layered glass of the thermal window creating the effect.

Brian knew that, as an orderly, his focus belonged on his superior, eyes in contact or downcast. He avoided looking out again toward the drought-faded autumn oaks and maples as the staff therapist debriefed him. Clinicians specializing in autism are hyperaware of gaze protocol, and violations would be noted in employee files. He was expected to act like a respectful participant in the healing process after the CareWell Behavioral Analysis and Remediation Institute lost another client. An urge to spit on the thick beige carpet next to the therapist's ivory pumps churned at the edge of Brian's mind.

She patted his fingers, her polished nails lightly scraping his knuckles. "I hear Rowena liked you. She didn't like many of us here."

Brian pulled his hand away as politely as he could and rubbed the buzz-cut stubble at the back of his leathery neck. He'd kept the severe trim from when he'd left the service a couple of decades before. "Ro was a wanderer. She wasn't really connected to any of us."

The therapist echoed his distant tone. "The pigmentation disfigurement, so sad, and only becoming more obvious. I know it was tedious for staff, the family insisting on the topical treatments.

Understandable, though, their hopes. She would have been a beautiful child."

Brian clenched his jaw. The hot-tempered nine-year-old's vitiligo never seemed to bother her, other than the twice-daily sensory affront of being slathered in heavily perfumed skin creams. Brian had avoided in-house training in therapeutic restraint techniques, pleading his bad back, and discreetly made sure not to be around for those medicinal applications. Rowena would target the glass jars with a wicked kick or slap to a staffer's ointment-slippery hand if she could.

The need to cover every inch of her with gunk had at least spared her being fitted with one of CareWell Behavioral's signature disciplinary shock harnesses. She hadn't been a biter when she'd arrived at the institute, but it didn't take her long to become one. She'd been razzed for her patchy skin by a few kids, but they weren't allowed much slack with the teasing. The senior staff reserved the bullying to themselves, nominally as part of her behavior modification plan.

It had taken Brian weeks to connect with her. Usually, new kids at the institute were drawn to him, but Rowena had given him the side-eye long after she'd had time to assure herself he'd respect her boundaries and aversions.

There eventually came a moment when Brian imagined offering to adopt her. He knew it wasn't realistic with his income and living situation, but no kid at the institute had touched him as strongly. In late spring, he'd noticed Rowena spending her rare good-behavior tokens on a stuffed pony from a clinic vending kiosk, and he told her she was marked like a palomino. She did look something like that, with a ragged, paler blaze against the fair skin of her face from forehead to chin, tattered albino gloves and socks, and a pure white off-center streak like a forelock in her blonde hair. She'd stared into the corner with a beaming smile and flapped her mottled hands at the idea.

That hard-won bond had been broken by autumn. She'd become withdrawn after her treatment protocol had been revised. Specified staff could talk to her only if she addressed them with proper speech, not just sounds and gestures, and no electronic assistance. Forcing clients to overcome challenges with spoken language was one of the prime directives of the institute, which defined ultimate success as making its clients indistinguishable from their non-autistic peers.

When Rowena had tugged Brian's arm and mimed entering

phrases on her confiscated tablet, he'd shaken his head. He needed to keep his job.

At the time, the therapist who now sat in front of him had said, "Ten months here is long enough to wean herself from that communication device. We know she's made attempts at verbal speech in the past. She has words. She can start using them."

By Christmas, Rowena had been found dead of exposure behind overgrown shrubbery in the old section of the grounds. All because she found it easier to speak through her fingers, and she wouldn't be bullied. Brian's tears over that had been silent and private, rather than the pro forma public sniffles senior staff displayed.

Brian stole another glance at the window and kept his thoughts to himself.

The therapist's smile congealed. "So, then, nothing to go over? No concerns—no I-should-have-dones?"

"No, ma'am, not—not unless...unless you think—"

"You did everything according to her protocols, Brian. So. Other business. We've put another client into the active measures aversives program. When you return from your hunting trip..." she shivered, with a disapproving scowl, "...you'll be connecting with his teachers to ensure it goes seamlessly." She handed him a digital clipboard with the new guidelines.

Brian's expression blanked. Kids who wore the battery-powered shock harnesses would obsessively scan every move of the designated staff. High-level staffers who worked directly with clients wore a set of laminated ID photos of aversive-fitted children dangling at their waists. Each photo was connected to a remote button which could unleash the punishment. It was advertised to parents as harmless, but one of Brian's duties was to tend to burns on arms, legs, and backs caused by the equipment.

Brian cleared his throat softly. "May I ask why, Dr. Pratt? He seems like a good kid."

The senior therapist's mouth twisted into an unctuously sorrowful smirk. "He's started refusing to use his words and physically resisting facilitated eye contact...and worse, he's begun to self-harm, Brian. You know we can't permit that."

* * *

As he made for the exit at the end of his shift, Brian reminded himself to slow his pace through the galleria. He'd seen the shadow in the woods, and he felt something waiting there. It had been in his dreams recently, a thing he vaguely remembered his sleeping brain calling the Broker, that could be bargained with in ways that weren't fathomable to his waking mind. Concentrating on making his walk smooth and even, he stifled a sense of urgency. His sciatic limp drew attention even when he wasn't trying to rush. Management disapproved of movement that could be read as unease, particularly in quasi-public areas.

The reward mall was the outward face of the facility, and visitors were permitted at any hour. Clients redeemed their good-behavior vouchers at the gaudy arcades and vendors whose endlessly looping jangles echoed in the long corridor. He avoided the stares of the larger-than-life animatronic plastic characters from *Alice in Wonderland*, forcing himself into a dignified gait that jarred his fused lower spine but would be more acceptable to the omnipresent cameras.

Suddenly, a human-sized albino rabbit with back-lit red eyes scooted past on its track, squeakily muttering, "I'm late," with out-of-synch mouth movements. Brian shuddered as the thing lurched around the corner at the far end of the hall, back to the blocks from which it would launch itself at another randomly determined interval. He'd never gotten used to it.

The staff apparently found his exaggerated startle response more amusing than worrisome. His performance reviews were good, despite the standard-issue bevy of ghosts that followed him as a combat veteran. Brian had his bad dreams and hair-trigger reflexes, but the labels and their consequences were worse. He was careful to avoid confiding anything to anyone that would put *Suspected PTSD* in his file.

He was better prepared for the ticking noise that followed, and the cheerfully threatening female voice saying, "Remember, kids, be ready and show up on time. You never know what might happen if you're tardy. Off with his head! Ha! Ha!"

Brian resisted the urge to mouth sarcastically along with the words that had been drilled into his brain through countless repetitions. Rowena had shared those silent jokes, snickering behind her hand. He'd come to trust her not to betray him when he'd mimicked senior staff. To the therapists, she only said, in her digitized voice, "Mr. Nicholas is always nice," and once that voice was taken from her, she never said anything again.

After the change in Rowena's protocol, Brian had treated her like a behaviorist's black box—a subject without an inner life—the way the institute expected of its employees. It twisted his guts to do it. She'd never be indistinguishable from other kids her age, no matter how many hours of modification drills she was put through, her sharp little teeth kept at a safe distance from her tormentors by a padded chair restraint that came down over her shoulders like a roller coaster harness. Somehow, Rowena had managed to keep her sense of self, bruised but intact, through her last act of defiance.

Unseen, she'd crossed the wide, serpentine drive that divided the modern, multi-facility complex from the disused cluster of crumbling Victorian institutional buildings. The sweeping phalanx of cameras on the pedestrian walkway bridging the drive hadn't picked her up. Elopers who knew what they were doing avoided them, and Rowena had been savvy beyond her years about evading authority.

She'd never left the grounds. Her body was curled against the cut-stone foundation of the shuttered edifice usually called the old administration building. Every nook of the building's wings, used as storage, had been checked. Mountains of document boxes, office furniture, and rusted air conditioners were carefully probed. There was no sign she'd gone inside, though she'd been slight enough to slip past the plywood barriers. Brian had suggested asking the state police for assistance in the search, but the idea was shot down as not showing the facility in a good light. The senior staff had said the cameras were sufficient.

Rowena's final choice had been to lie down against the foot of the neo-Gothic hulk and let it drain her of life. The granite, instead of offering shelter, seemed to have sucked the warmth out of her. The night had been cold, but she'd died quickly even so.

* * *

It wasn't until he drove under the Taconic Behavioral Health Complex sign on the walkway that Brian felt he could take in a good, clean breath. The eastern escarpment of the mountain range the complex was named for loomed ahead, subtly colored as an antique tapestry. Low, steely clouds raced in its airstream, harbingers of a front laden with early, wet snow. Hawks lofted in the current, hunting ahead of him. For now, the clear late afternoon opened overhead into a vault of sapphire space deep enough to make out a star or two.

Tension dropped from his shoulders. He was headed home. Not the battered mobile home he shared with a deaf cat on the wooded lot he'd inherited from his father, but home to those mountains. The scent of snow-dampened leaves and dark loam, the rush of an icy stream, birdcalls and wind-rustles, and the silence, sweetest of all. Tonight he'd eat for the physical challenges ahead, spend a few hours watching the satellite-fed television with old Moe on his lap if the weather didn't mess up the signal, and turn out the lights early.

The drive took over an hour. Beyond the pampered farms that ringed the galleries, craft-collectives, and antique shops of town, the landscape changed. In the steeper, rockier foothills were working woodlots, leaner farms with older paint, and tracts of scrubland so used up it would be decades before nature healed them. Brian's trailer was up a half-mile of narrow, washboarded gravel road flanked by thickets of unmanaged saplings about as big around as a man's forearm and far taller than they'd be if they didn't have to fight each other for the sun.

The logging company that put the road in was long gone. The county graded often enough to keep trees from growing in the right-of-way, but beyond that, Brian and the few others who lived along it were on their own. Aside from the ever-changing occupants of the wannabe hipster homestead on the one lot with a decent view, the neighbors were longtime residents.

The view place, with its passive solar heat and kit-built greenhouse, was partly owned by an institute speech therapist whom Brian sometimes gave a ride to work when mountain storms made the roads treacherous. Their conversations on the trip were limited to talking about their pets, particularly after Brian showed her a photo of what he called his calendar boy. "Mr. December" was his glistening white, longhaired, aquamarine-eyed cat, sitting on a sunlit windowsill with blurred, sparkling snow behind him. His co-worker had taken the phone from Brian's hand with a squee, and since then, Moe was all she asked about. Nothing else Brian had to say was of much interest to his foul-weather passenger unless she needed his help, but she appeared to understand the value of keeping on his good side.

He'd shown the picture to Rowena too, and she'd entered her own word for Moe on her tablet. The synthesized voice called him Crystal Cat. She'd once said, "Crystal Cat doesn't hear. I don't talk. Two sides of silence."

Brian knew how to operate a snowplow, could fix most things that might go wrong with an old car, his family had been in the area for more than a century, and he'd been an Army medic. He had a beautiful cat. Up that road, he was a respected, valued member of the community.

* * *

By eight o'clock, sleet was collecting in the satellite dish, scattering the TV signal. Cold air leaked in around the aluminum-framed windows. Brian pulled out the laser pointer and played with Moe for a while, then gathered his gear and provisions for morning on the tiny kitchen table. Licenses and an antlered deer tag went in the holster bag he'd wear under his vest and jacket, along with an Android phone with a powerful antenna, once he blew the omnipresent cat hair out of the waterproof zippered compartment. Moe's hair could get into seemingly impossible places.

Brian finished putting the few dishes away and gave the linoleum a quick sweep. Moe seemed needy, weaving and rubbing against his legs, leaving more hair on his black sweatpants. Brian stretched out on the claw-shredded couch and let the cat snuggle under his chin. Moe pressed against the vibrations from Brian's larynx, purring into their shared warm space.

Brian murmured, "Hey, buddy. Krysta from up the road is gonna check in on you tomorrow, and probably the day after. Don't give me the *look*, you spoiled beast—I can't exactly take you along."

He scratched the cat's back, thinking of when he'd picked up the emaciated, too-young-to-wean kitten from the side of the road on his way home from work a dozen years before. The vet bills had stretched his budget thin. He wondered for the hundredth time where he'd be if he hadn't had to pay off those credit cards.

Moe laid a paw against Brian's face and purred louder.

Brian turned his head and made a soft spitting sound to get the fine, clinging fur away from his mouth. "Never saw myself having a cat. Worthless animals—particularly you. You can't even find a mouse unless you smell him."

Moe headbutted Brian under the chin hard enough to make his teeth click together.

"Yeah, I hear ya. I'm an asshole."

The cat had been named in honor of Brian's emotional support canine, partly because his loud, rounded meow sounded like "Moe." A veterans' charity called Through the Darkness had issued him the black Labrador mix when he'd returned from his last tour of duty, while he still lived in the city. Brian had lost the first Moe to cancer a few years later.

Moe the First had always been a good boy, ignoring other dogs who wanted to play, no matter how they teased him. One of Brian's most intrusive memories was of the only time he'd taken him to an off-leash park. Too inconsequential to mention to a counselor, but he couldn't get the incident to fade off. It had been after one of Moe's last veterinary treatments. Any ordinary animal would have been cranky and snappish, but the dog had been the level-headed one, doing his job keeping Brian steady.

A big husky mix had charged up, reared back, and tossed something high, snatching it from the air and shaking it, then slackening its jaws almost, but not quite wide enough to drop the plaything to the ground. Its wicked grin seemed to dare Moe to snatch the flopping thing away. As Brian had focused, he realized the treasured toy was a live squirrel, limp with shock, and every snap of the dog's head sent a few drops of red spattering into the rubber mulch. The looping scene could get more distressing than the combat footage usually on replay in his brain.

Now Brian fiddled with the charity's scarab emblem pin on Moe's cat collar that he'd transferred from the dog's harness. "You stuck it out until your poor old dog-body couldn't hold up anymore, and still your job wasn't done. I'm just as much of an ungrateful bastard as I ever was."

He held the cat's face gently between his hands, looking into Moe's intensely blue eyes. "Yeah, I knew it was you from the time you were dribbling formula out the sides of your mouth. I'm starting to get it, I think, Mr. Crystal. Of course, you'd have to kill me if you told me how it works."

Moe stretched, and Brian smoothed his back. "You'd be better off if something did happen, old buddy. You could leave for finer things while you still have your looks. I think your babysitter's hoping to end up with you somehow, but you better make your move soon. I haven't told her how you can't hear yourself, so you scream like a freight train just for the hell of it."

* * *

Brian moved restlessly in his dream. He followed a black retriever through a dim forest, calling, "Slow up, Moe. I don't get it yet, buddy, and my back's killing me."

The dog turned back, gazing into him with infinitely soft brown eyes, and then trotted on, disappearing into the murk as Brian fell behind. Moe would never leave him unless it was important.

A ticking sound filled the woods like an anxious pulse. Something moved near a break in the trees. It had an autistic gait, running on tiptoes with bent elbows, hands flopping. He called to it, but it broke for the clearing and vanished. In its place, a hot, dark thing breathed in a wilderness of traps. It had something limp and bloody in its mouth, offering a trade. Brian thrashed himself partly awake before being pulled back in.

He drove through the gateway formed by the Taconic complex bridge, the vault of stars overhead. Instead of the afternoon sun, an immense winter moon shone on the drive so brightly it sparkled. The cratered orb seemed near enough to touch. Gigantic animals paced in the shadows beside the road.

His truck faded and was gone. He walked along the fancy farms where he'd found the kitten. This was a world that discarded any undesirable creatures it bred, maybe from cars, maybe from a house nearby.

Something unseen tugged at his arm, wailing wordlessly to him in a childish voice. It needed something from him. There might be a deal to be made here, a way to a fair exchange. What Brian would offer had to be worth the thing he wanted. The game's machinery was vast, but he was working toward understanding. The barrier felt full of potential. It was a likely place, but the Broker hadn't arrived. In the distance, the ticking sound echoed.

Cool moonlight clearing his head, Brian realized he'd run from what he was looking for back in the forest, and cursed his own cowardice. The Broker had come and gone.

He started looking in the tall grass along the ditch, thinking he might catch up to Moe that way if Moe was tracking someone between realms.

The road surface sank into the earth, and the moon and its glow ebbed away. He put his hands out to find his path, stumbling over the uneven ground, touching things he couldn't quite see.

A glowing-eyed, doppler-distorted, screeching wail passed him, lurching and surging. "I'm laa...ate..."

Brian reached for his rifle, but he'd forgotten to bring it.

* * *

Sunrise scattered the fog from Brian's brain. He'd been hiking for nearly an hour, but the tinge of fiery dawn light catching a distant ridge brought him to full attention. Scents of loam and fading bracken frosted with ice from yesterday's sleet came up from his bootsteps. Clouds of his breath rose into the pinkish-gray early morning sky.

He'd left the trailhead parking lot far behind, the few hunters there still drinking coffee in their warm trucks. Most of those wouldn't ford the wide stream at the base of the mountain, never venturing into the fretwork of small, swift brooks above.

Breathing deep, Brian could forget everything outside earshot. There was only the grating sound of crow squabbles echoing in the ravine. Nothing beyond that mattered. Time to forget the institute and its shadows, and Rowena tugging at his arm. He remembered her touching the photograph of Mr. Crystal and smiled, thinking of Moe's squawking, unmusical voice, and then he put the thought aside. Whatever the cat's interdimensional navigational skills might be, Brian now had to deal with one hard reality—the potential consequences of any mistakes committed after entering the wilderness alone.

Diverging from the main trail running parallel to the wide stream, he checked his GPS compass, marked his paper map, and attended to where he put his feet and trekking pole as he descended the steep slope. In the spring of a wet year, the meltwater would make a roaring torrent, but in a dry autumn like this one, he needed to be mindful that the vanished currents might have carved treacherous voids hidden by debris.

He paused on a ledge to note a heraldic-looking mummified crow with partly open obsidian wings. It lay on its back in the frozen leaves, its clean-picked breast revealing whitened ribs. Its ice-spangled head was turned to the side, crook-necked, as if it had met its fate swooping in too quickly for a drink, its eyes hollow and dry after the forest's custodians had gleaned its half-seen skull.

Registering the lesson, Brian jumped warily across the flat rocks poking above the water to the narrower trail beyond.

* * *

Tiny, bright crystals swirled in the air, obscuring the far edge of the high clearing in a glistening haze. The midday sun cut briefly through the fast-moving clouds, just enough to confirm time and direction. Brian felt more alive than he had in months. Years ago, his father had taken him to this high meadow when it had been baited with illegal salt licks. Now he watched for deer coming to browse tender saplings and the last grasses before they went dormant under the snow.

Brian remembered how his father had taught him in whispers as they hid in the brush for hours of his childhood. He'd learned how the forest had been stolen from the Mohicans, and how good citizens continued to benefit from that and other incomprehensibly vast historical crimes. When he'd gone into the military, he'd seen that machinery in action, and had come back to find the lines he'd had to his old life didn't connect anymore. His father was dead, and no one else from his past could engage him. He had a hard time holding a job. The sister he barely spoke to had finally dragged him to the charity that issued him Moe the First.

Moe was trained to recognize the scent of stress, the twitches and rumbles humans didn't register until too late. Every time he recognized the triggers, Moe would nudge and paw and whimper and get slapped away. The dog would keep up being an annoyance until Brian relented, embracing Moe's sturdy neck, muttering some variant of, "Twenty grand and a year of training to get you to learn how to be the biggest pain in the ass money could buy." He'd breathe in the smell of coarse, clean fur as shivers of unnamable emotion emptied into the fathomless well of Moe's devotion.

After Moe died, Brian went back to the hunting camp his father had left him in the Taconics. The employment offer from the institute was good, and he wanted to try to communicate with the kids who ended up calling him Mr. Nicholas, the ones who tugged at his arm, pleading for more than the rules said he could give. A nine-year-old who loved ponies and wanted her confiscated tablet back.

He blinked away the shadow.

Now he needed to forget all that. The mountain was what it was, and he had just put three rounds of ammunition into a lethal weapon.

A flicker of motion caught in his binoculars. Brian reached for his rifle. What he saw through the scope made his breath sharpen and his hands shake. Stark against the treeline at the edge of the meadow, a rare piebald six-point buck stood at alert, sniffing the wind. It appeared pure white, but as Brian steadied the rifle, he saw a spatter of dun-colored blotches along the animal's neck and shoulders, and the dark of its eye and nose. He'd never been a trophy sportsman, but now he trembled with the rush from a chance given few hunters in a lifetime.

As he strove to steady his aim, the deer pawed the ground slowly and bobbed its head, aware of danger. Adrenaline made Brian giddy; he knew what was happening, still the surge washed over his rational thoughts. It was too late to set up the kill properly, but the animal was going to bolt. As the buck snorted and wheeled, he squeezed off a shot. A less experienced hunter would have missed, and it would have been a better thing.

The buck bleated like a fawn and trotted awkwardly into the woods with its back arched. The composted-hay scent of paunch carried on a swirl of wind. Brian cursed himself bitterly. Whitetail hunters' lore was full of admonitions about animals hit in the stomach. His father had warned him of what must be done if he ever inflicted that unworthy wound.

He'd grown up knowing a gut shot meant the tenderloins, the best of the meat, would be spoiled. Worse, a beautiful creature would die a slow, agonizing death. If Brian could avoid losing him, he'd be lucky. The deer would seek a safe place to bed down, where it would gradually go into septic shock if left undisturbed. His father had warned him to wait until nightfall to begin tracking to avoid scaring the buck deeper into the forest, losing all chance to salvage any part of it or save it from more hours of suffering.

* * *

Brian slept uneasily, sitting sheltered in the hollow of a tree. He'd drifted off, worrying he was making a poor choice. His father had never had to deal with big predators in the forest. He'd learned those rules before eastern coyotes had come to fill in the void left by the wolves and bears that had been driven out along with the People of the Waters. The stories he'd learned with his father were told when they had no competition for prey. The buck might be taken down by another predator before he found it.

As Brian's dream took hold, he wondered if he had a bargain to make. The Broker paced unseen, dark and vast, awaiting his offer. The same uncannily close moon hung low, and the ticking sound resonated from it, amplified as if the orb were hollow metal. The buck was bedding underneath the overgrown shrubbery against the foundation of the old administration building. That meant Rowena might still be wandering in the liminal spaces. There was a chance she could yet be taken back from the cold darkness.

There was a brook between Brian and the buck, and he teetered on the slippery rocks as he crossed, but the brook kept widening. The barrier was stretching and flexing. If he could kill the buck honorably and offer it, a transaction was perhaps possible. Rowena was worthy of a piebald buck racked with agony. She'd borne her own pain until it grew so heavy she'd left it in the freezing stone. It could be a fair trade, but Brian didn't know how to reach the Broker. He wanted to ask Moe. Moe would know, but he wasn't there.

* * *

The phone alarm cut through, jolting Brian out of the dream. His mind spun with how to field-dress, quarter, and carry the carcass out if it wasn't too contaminated. The longer the search, the more toxins would circulate in the buck's bloodstream. The beautiful coloration would leave a pelt ordinary as a cow's without the regal form underneath it, but there wasn't time or energy to carry it out intact for a taxidermist, and no money for that on an orderly's salary. The head as a trophy would be the best part, but would only remind Brian of how deeply he'd failed.

The gibbous moon was clear enough to see by, if not quite as large and glaucous as the one in his dreams. There was unmelted snow in the shadows of the woods, and the hoofprints and blood drops shouldn't be hard to follow. He walked to the point where the deer had been wounded, and looked back carefully at the way he'd come to orient himself.

Contrary to myth, wounded deer don't always go downhill or to water, but Brian decided that wouldn't be a bad place to start. He reminded himself to watch for coyote traps set by other hunters more aggressive about dealing with the competition. He sighed at the dried splash of greenish ichor and blood on a flat stone at the field's edge and walked silently into the night forest.

* * *

The buck was curled on the flood-leveled sand between the exposed roots of a massive hemlock holding to the far cliff bank of a small brook, opposite its giant twin on the closer side. The animal seemed to glow in the moonlight, its coat was so pale. That it had lived to adulthood with markings that conspicuous was evidence of its savvy.

Brian crossed the trickle noiselessly and approached by inches, aware of the sound of his breathing. There was coyote scat along the top of the bank; it was unlikely the buck would have sheltered there unless it was closing in on the end. Its belly was distended, and a putrid smell hung over it.

Carefully, Brian knelt next to the animal. Its eyes were shut, and its breath was faint. He touched its ear and felt the cold in it. The ear twitched, and the buck's large black eye opened for a moment, almost disinterested. Leaning over it, he whispered, "I'm sorry. God, so sorry." He swung his rifle around for a coup de grace, but before he could set up the shot in the short white fur of the deer's forehead, it opened its mouth, heaved its last, deepest sigh, and was gone.

Brian slumped his back against the bank, his boots in the shallow water. He closed his eyes, arched his neck, clenched his fists, and let out a dry sob. The knife he needed was at his hip. If there was any meat to be saved, if the animal's death was to have meaning, he had to open it up to dress it. Fighting back flickers of battlefield memories, he prepared himself for the task. He didn't have strength left to hoist the carcass shoulder-height to the top of the bank, so it had to be done down on the drought-exposed shoal next to the water. The moon hung between the towering twin evergreens, illuminating his work.

Blood from the slit throat sank into the wet sand and darkened the stream. Brian swallowed hard and shook the shadows from his head. From there, the cuts came easier, made with the automatic care of a man used to butchering what he killed. The stench when he opened the abdomen made him gag, but he focused and continued.

There was a splash, and a soft, musical growl. Brian stiffened and turned slowly away from his work. At least seven eastern coyotes circled on the banks, tall, lanky juveniles staring down and sniffing, and two large adults, likely their parents, below in the stream. One of those, the darker of the two, paced with a slight limp as if from a long-healed wound.

The rifle was behind Brian, tucked safe and out of easy reach up in the roots, and to use the knife would be to invite being attacked by the full pack. These coywolves were the new wolves of the Appalachian deep woods, adapted to the void left by their predecessors. They had bastard remnants of the ancient order in their genes, and had grown more formidable than their foxlike trickster western cousins. Domestic canine blood had also been drawn up into their genetic tree, and their understanding of humans gave them a near-uncanny edge in the constant conflict for primacy in the forest. Coywolves were unlikely to kill a human, but to take on a clan of them with a skinning knife was a good way to test the odds.

Brian crouched and turned toward the massive sable-black adult male, holding the knife low in front of himself. The scar of a leghold trap marked one of its front paws where it had slid its own skin off to escape, leaving a crude sleeve of hardened tissue as if its lower leg had been held in a flame. The animal's yellow eyes and clean-fanged grin caught the light. Its breath was like summer roadkill when the sun beats down after a heavy rain. The female, lithe and lighter-colored, sniffed at the deer carcass. Brian made a slight, involuntary moan of protest. The father lunged, clamping his jaws around Brian's wrist through his jacket.

It felt for a moment like the coywolf might release him, but he was only setting himself for a deeper bite. Brian heard a meaty crunch as tendons split in his forearm. He slashed at the animal's neck. It let go to defend itself, teeth gnashing at his face, and then vanished.

Brian reeled. He had to get to his backpack. Antiseptic, an emergency dose of antibiotic, sutures, and a firm dressing on the wound. He avoided the feeding group tugging and tearing at the carcass, shoving at each other for access to the choicest parts. His knife ready, he slowly pulled at the knapsack resting on a massive root a few feet from them, but the bloody-faced canines barely noticed him. The rifle was too close to the snarling swarm to risk the reach.

* * *

The yips of lower-caste juveniles fighting for scraps echoed upstream. Brian finished dressing the punctures in his wrist and forearm, pulling the roll of gauze with his teeth as he wrapped it. He watched for the pack patriarch. The others hadn't shown much interest in him, but the leader wasn't anywhere Brian could see, and that made his back prickle. Carefully, he re-packed his emergency kit by the light of a tiny LED, and saw Moe had left a few long white hairs among the neatly wrapped amulets of sanitation there.

A muffled growl on the bank above knotted his stomach. Forcing himself to look up, Brian shuddered. Looming against the night sky, the sable coywolf seemed even larger, tossing something high in the air and shaking it in a nauseatingly familiar way. Except the limp animal was a white cat. The Broker was challenging Brian to play.

Brian screamed, "NO! I will hunt you down and gut you alive if you hurt him, whatever the hell you are!"

The Broker whip-snapped his prize hard enough to throw it across the stream. The body slapped down in front of Brian. He gathered the cat into his arms, feeling for vital signs, but even as his fingers sought a pulse, the thing he held became a lifeless object—a filthy, waterlogged stuffed toy. A palomino pony.

Brian's hands shook too hard to hold the thing. It dropped to the wet sand and sank through, out of sight. There was nothing on the high bank. The carcass of the buck lay on the shoal, undisturbed. The tang of blood and sepsis still hung in the air, but the deer appeared whole, undamaged. It twitched.

Sightless eyes unblinking, the buck staggered to its feet. It bleated painfully, the echoing sound teasing Brian's memory, filling in what might not be there. "Laaa…laa…aate."

Seizing the chance, Brian slung his knapsack on his back, dashed across the stream, and reached for his rifle, coming within feet of the buck. The animal paused as if sensing something near, then tottered and collapsed a few steps from where it had lain.

Brian froze, holding the rifle by the barrel in his swollen, aching left hand. A chilly glow silhouetted the branches overhead, the moon washing over the deer's snow-white flank. A movement like breathing, but not quite, disturbed its belly. Something was pushing against it from inside. The knife was in Brian's grip before he was conscious of it, but he couldn't think to pull it from the sheath and move the blade with purpose. He stepped back and gaped.

The thing inside the buck swelled, splitting it open. When the crouching figure emerged, it left a void in the carcass as black as deep space.

The rifle dropped to the sand. "Rowena!"

The child whimpered, her mottled gray skin cold to Brian's touch as he reached out. She rested her head against his shoulder. Her hair had the same gory smell as everything surrounding her, but it was dry, and strands of it pulled away as Brian stroked her head.

Rowena tugged on his arm.

He said, "I don't have your tablet, sweetheart. We can get you another one."

She tugged harder, her grasp icy and powerful.

Brian stepped back, but couldn't free himself. Rowena made a gurgling sound. He tried to yank his arm out of her grip, and she stared at him, her face full of chill fury.

"I'm sorry, Ro. I know. I should have fought harder, should have let the damned job go."

Rowena's eyes were black with rage. She opened her mouth slowly. It was full, and a drip of fetid paunch pooled on her lip and dribbled down her chin.

Brian shoved her away with his full strength. She fell back into the brook without making a splash, and was gone. The water slipped over the spot where she sank into the streambed.

The drought-throttled trickle flowed on, snaking its way down the mountain.

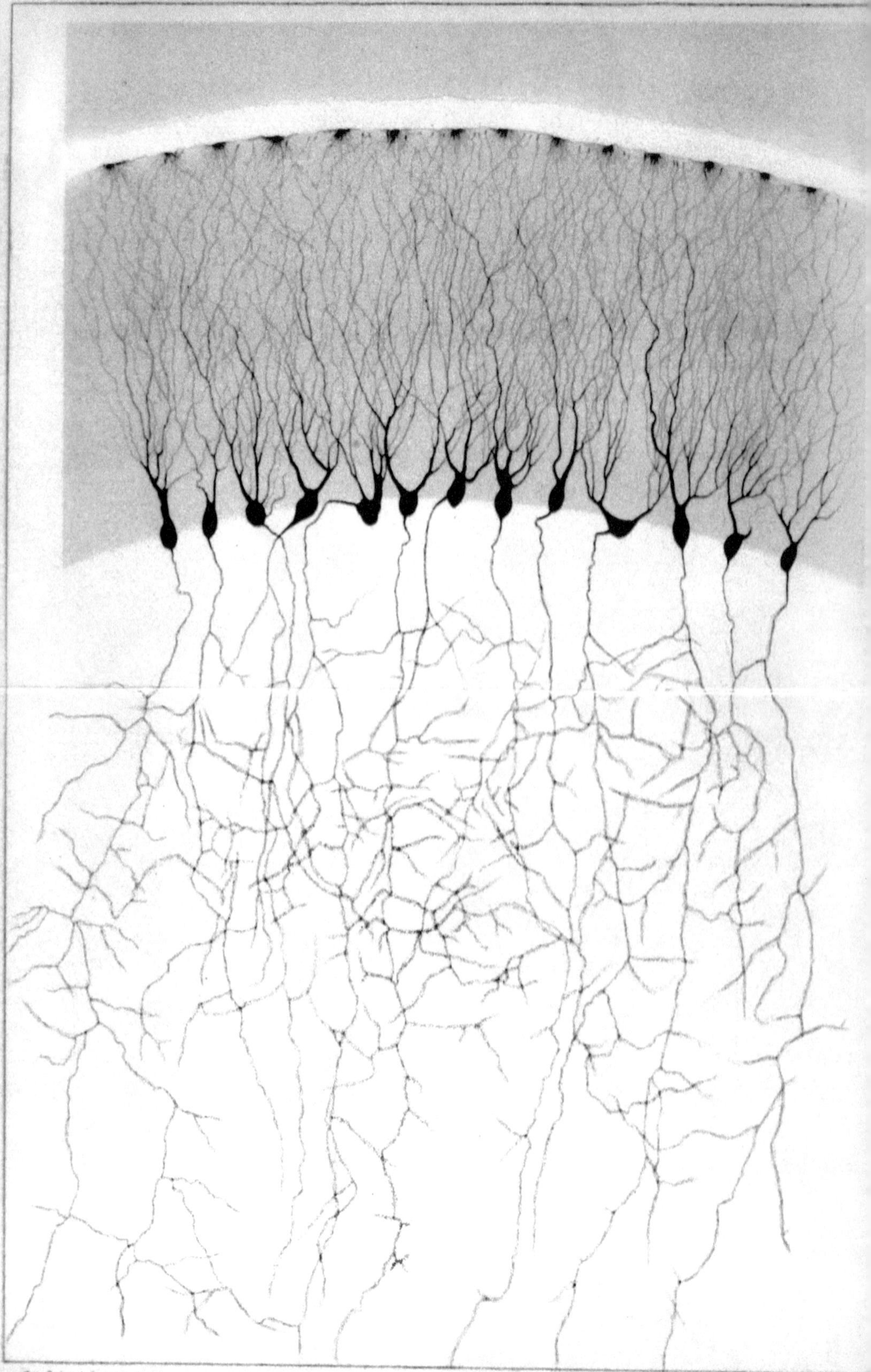

P.A. Ogheri inc

Lit. Vares

THE RED KING

'And if he left off dreaming about you, where do you suppose you'd be?'

'Where I am now, of course,' said Alice.

'Not you!' Tweedledee retorted contemptuously. 'You'd be nowhere. Why, you're only a sort of thing in his dream!'

'If that there King was to wake,' added Tweedledum, 'you'd go out—bang!— just like a candle!'

—Lewis Carroll, *Through the Looking-Glass*

The revenant cluster contemplated Dr. Hamish Fallowfield as he scanned the night-vision monitors for client movement. If he was aware of being the subject of another level of surveillance, he ignored it. Perhaps he'd noticed an indistinct shadow without a light source or felt the hairs on his arm rise. The bitter-smelling steam from his coffee mug could account for a shimmering distortion in the air near his face.

An hour earlier, when the weariest part of the day had settled in, he'd been startled by what had looked like a huge, awkward black bird standing in the corner of his office, holding a sack in its beak from which spilled corroded coins. He'd pulled himself up sharply and cleared the sleep from his eyes to recognize his own antique-brass-buttoned coat hanging on the rack in in the corner. In that momentary flush of fear, the cluster had slipped into his mind, and now it watched from both outside and in.

Fallowfield stood behind the night security personnel, each seated before the monitors for eight private client rooms and a section of hallway. The dozen workers sat along a U-shaped desk in a large, bright room. The monitor array was the facility's promise to parents and guardians. They could rely on hierarchical layers of constant supervision over their children. Any abuse of clients would be seen, recorded, and dealt with.

Clients were permitted to adjust their sleeping positions, and continent ones were allowed to use the toilet after notifying staff via intercom. Any other motion was considered noncompliant. Fallowfield was director of the facility, and those were his rules. The CareWell Behavioral Analysis and Remediation Institute, crown jewel of the Taconic Behavioral Health Center complex, was renowned for its success in training autistic juveniles to pass as non-neurodivergent. No augmentative and alternative communication devices were allowed except during therapy sessions. According to the director's rules, clients must learn to speak in a socially acceptable fashion or else go unheard. They would be trained to be indistinguishable from their non-autistic peers. Despite onerous tuition costs, the institute had a deep waiting list.

The clustered awareness drew in to a more intense observation of a handsome, forty-ish, white-coated woman next to Fallowfield. She leaned over a staffer's shoulder and picked up the microphone by his arm. "Miles, please stop rocking yourself. It's eleven o'clock, past time for you to lie down and be still."

In the eye of the infrared camera, the lanky teenager caught sitting on his bed twitched. He stared up at the speaker in his room, his features smudged in the blurry greenish image on the screen. He wailed and fluttered his fingers.

The woman said, "Miles. Stop. Quiet hands. We understand this is a stressful time, but you'll have to adjust."

Miles hit his forearm with a balled fist and snarled, and the white-coated woman shrank back.

Fallowfield moved in, assessing the escalating conflict without interceding.

The woman's eyes narrowed. "Miles! Use your words! Apologize immediately! You sound like an animal. NO self-harming!"

Miles awkwardly raised a middle finger in the darkness. The woman reached to press a button on the monitor console. Miles made an anguished howl as he reached for his ankle, tugging at a plastic-shielded apparatus affixed to it by a sturdy strap.

Fallowfield put his hand out for the microphone. "Miles, this is Dr. Fallowfield. This is precisely why you were fitted with the device. Now you've learned firsthand what it's for, I hope we won't have to use it again. We can't have regression here. We have to put a stop to this, Miles."

Miles's panicked voice echoed, "Put a stop to this, Miles."

The cluster slipped out of Fallowfield's mind and tried to comfort the boy, but humans needed calm and quiet to perceive the kindness of such entities. The institution in all its forms would ensure no inmate it held would ever know peace. The same script had been acted out in this room and all the rooms like it in the history of the institution. There would be no mercy here, because there never was.

Miles started humming quietly, and got another jolt.

Fallowfield said, "No echolalia. You're fifteen. There's no excuse for that at your age, and there's no excuse for this infantile self-soothing. Now, apologize to Dr. Rivers, please."

Miles froze, stammering. "Apologize...Dr. Rivers."

Fallowfield frowned. "You'll have to do better than that, Miles. Dr. Rivers is waiting."

Miles gasped and swallowed. "Dr. Rivers...I'm...sorry. I will...do better."

The cluster dissipated with a grieving, soundless sigh.

* * *

Fallowfield savored the aftertaste of Kelli Rivers' brief but unmistakable display of feminine deference as he'd complimented her handling of her first shock administration. He was pleased with his choice to make her the new supervisor of the third-shift staff. Kelli was too old to arouse him, though she presented herself well, and hiring her had been a coup. She'd been courted by clinics and university programs across the country, but she'd chosen his facility because of the purity of its behaviorist protocols.

Checking himself in his full-length office mirror, Fallowfield speculated as to whether his patrician features and distinguished bearing might have influenced Kelli's choice of employers. At the late hour, he sported a slightly loosened tie and shirtsleeves neatly rolled to the forearm to convey vitality and engagement in the work.

Fallowfield opened an anonymous browser and signed into his private email account. The cluster moved forward like a school of fish, gliding into his murky shallows. He looked around the room for something to account for his prickling skin, and decided it was a draft from the cold front moving in. His inbox showed two new items. One was from the mother of the current star client at the facility, the seventeen-year-old model known by her first name, Sybille. The second was from his attorney, regarding information he'd need to provide for a state inspection.

He sighed and relaxed into his high-backed cognac leather executive chair to open the first message.

Sybille Ranks' wealthy mother apparently thought since Fallowfield had given her his private address, her flirtation was welcome. It was, but only so much as toleration of it ensured steady support of the facility's endowment and the continued presence of her daughter in Fallowfield's custody. He released an annoyed sigh.

Beautiful Sybille had been adopted as a Russian orphan. At first, she seemed magical to her adoptive mother, who feared being labeled too old by the agency, however many bribes she paid. The white-blonde girl offered by the orphanage had been nearly three, not the infant Mrs. Ranks had hoped for, but lovely in a something-strange-about-it way. She wasn't hyper and needy like most children her age. Indeed, she barely walked unless coaxed, and expressed little interest in her new mother's attention.

Slowly, the reality of Sybille's silence, and the neurology behind it, revealed why it had been so easy to get her out of the country. After a few months, the alabaster-skinned toddler's wordlessness couldn't be explained by language differences and shyness in a new environment. Her refusal to eat anything but potatoes and bread was more than just homesickness for orphanage food. The way she stared without acknowledging anyone else made clear there was something inescapably wrong. Mrs. Ranks had spared no expense in seeking out cures and therapies for her daughter, but only when she'd found Fallowfield had Sybille become more tractable, even briefly holding eye contact.

Fallowfield closed the email, almost letting his mind wander too far into thoughts of that slender, pale body, and clicked on his lawyer's message.

The revenant cluster shuffled and churned. A leader seemed to be emerging from the communal consciousness. The collective consulted within itself.

Fallowfield opened his lawyer's note. It started out chattily, but after the first paragraph, the one that might be caught by the quick scan of a surveillance screening, it turned urgent.

The AG isn't dicking around on this, Hames. If you know what happened to those security cam records, you'd best tell me NOW. If I find out you've been holding back on me after I stuck my neck out telling the state investigation team you're clean, you're going to need new representation. They're acting like they know things I don't. Also, the files, Hames. I'm not liking how this is adding up. You were supposed to turn them over to my office six weeks ago. We can't mount a defense without knowing what's in them.

Fallowfield's stomach turned to writhing eels.

* * *

Fallowfield moved quietly down the darkened Looking-Glass Wonderland corridor. Its fake shops and kiosks based on Lewis Carroll's *Alice* books were the only place clients could redeem their good-behavior tokens. The checkerboard-floored galleria was silent, its life-sized animatronic figures frozen in place. Cameras covering it were motion-activated, but he had a master remote to keep them asleep.

Leaning on a pawn-shaped bollard by the shuttered Lair of the Jabberwocky, he double-checked the camera indicator lights. He entered and locked the door after himself. Several months before, he'd disabled the corridor cameras and a client had slipped out, following him. He struggled to recall the name of the nine-year-old, remembering only her disfiguring vitiligo and noncompliant attitude. Something about a Poe story... Ligeia... Rowena. That was it. Rowena. He vaguely regretted not becoming involved in the search for her. There were details he wished he'd been more on top of.

His outdoor coat made him sweat, but where he was going was unheated. He pulled out a small flashlight. Sharp shadows from the legs of the machines crossed the floor as he aimed the light low ahead of his feet. A whispering sound beside him made Fallowfield do a careful sweep of the wide room at floor level, and then a faster one of the tops of the machines and the life-sized, powered-off animatronic freaks lunging from the corners of the ceiling.

The hideous Duchess and Queen of Hearts were caught in mid-shriek, the Mad Hatter's eyes were frozen in a bulging roll with most of the iris lost up in his fiberglass skull, and the eponymous Jabberwock looked stunned in surprise, its mouth gaping and claws splayed. Something close to humiliation at being afraid in a room full of tacky ogres he'd designed himself burned in Fallowfield's cheeks.

* * *

Fallowfield took the maintenance corridor from the operator's room at the rear of the arcade. From there, he used the cramped, broiling-hot HVAC duct passage to the underground central utility complex. Skirting the perimeter of the fluorescent-lit warren where the walls turned from thickly painted cinderblock to brick and fieldstone, he sought the old foundation, full of gaps and brick-falls that released an earthy smell.

Behind a large set of metal lockers repurposed as utility storage, he squeezed into a concealed niche with a low, rusting metal door, spitting cobwebs away as he crouched to open it inward into darkness. The cramped entrance to the Antebellum-era tunnel belied the large space behind it. He'd learned of the tunnel from drawings he'd found when exploring the disused part of the grounds years before. Crumbling Victorian structures built of native granite housed countless brittle, discolored records along with the abandoned office furniture.

Fallowfield's flashlight caught foot-long limestone stalactites, their shadows gnashing with his hurried steps. Hiding from patrolling security staff, he was headed to the old administration building. No one could possibly know of the brass-handled file cabinet with the laptop hidden among the folders from when the place was called the Taconic State Hospital. This would have to be his last trip to his lair on the other end of the tunnel; there must be no trace for state inspectors to find.

* * *

The corridor seemed longer than Fallowfield remembered. His panting breath rose into the cold, musty air. The darkness stretched out in front and back of him farther than it should. Vague shapes that didn't accord with his memory loomed in the distance. Eyes deprived of light will make their own imagery, he reminded himself. Finally, the foundation of the old administration building appeared ahead. It seemed roughly as he remembered, although somehow larger.

Unlike the modern end, the Victorian terminus of the tunnel was framed by a portal worthy of it. The Gothic-arched rotted oak doors were open. On an early exploration when he was a couple decades younger, he'd forced them apart; now they loomed so massive, sagging on their corroded hinges, he couldn't imagine having the strength to move them.

Fallowfield entered the basement. The once-grand edifice above him was held up by a forest of junk-obscured masonry pillars that receded into shadows. Sweat chilled under his coat. Four huge furnace hulks covered in black dust lurked at the corners of the vast basement. He wondered how much coal they'd consumed to deliver enough steam to the upper floors.

Winter wind off the Taconic Mountains strafed the building. That was how Rowena had been found, dead of exposure up against the outside of the foundation. She must have followed him to this point, and then found an exit, going to ground snuggling the stone that sucked the heat out of her body.

He passed through the forest of columns, pushing his way through piles of trash, collapsing stacks of file boxes and unwieldy tangles of old furniture. Again, he felt as though he was traversing more space than his memory had mapped. The junk jungle seemed thicker, and it took an uncannily long time to fight his way to the stairs.

* * *

The mahogany door to the director's office glowed with sweet-smelling lemon-oil polish. The warm, quiet clinking of cast-iron radiators expanding with the pulse of steam through their veins filled the hall. Fallowfield ran his hand wonderingly over the wood panel and winced as his index finger came away with a dry splinter. He sucked it out, tasting blood and heavy dust—yet when he looked at the fingertip, it was rosy, clean and unharmed.

He cautiously gripped the burnished bronze knob, and flinched from an icy ache that reached into his arthritic joints. The door creaked open reluctantly, requiring some shoulder. The large office was empty, yet gaslight lamps flickered. He removed his coat and laid it on the chair behind the huge desk, rolling his sleeves up again for a look around.

Fallowfield's eyes danced over the glass-fronted bookshelves and anatomical models. His precious green-enameled steel file cabinet was there, but without rust or dents. The newest thing in the room, its Art Deco hardware shone, and the brass-bound leather top was a rich cordovan red-brown instead of cracked ash-gray. He started at the sound of sleeting rain against the tall, arched window behind the desk, and more so, the sheen of the clear, cold gibbous moon just above the horizon, and the powerful LED security lights of the guard station.

He glided over to a large, upright specimen case, unaware of having willed his feet to move there. Among the records in the file cabinet, he'd seen a black and white photograph of this nineteenth-century display in the old state hospital director's office. An engraved brass plate labeled its motionless citizens "The Seven Ages of Woman." The quality of the waxwork was breathtaking. The three rightmost, progressively aged nude figures were covered with bleached linen drapes, but the first four seemed to glow with a delicate life. Every hair had been individually set and the translucent skin hand-tinted with oils. The sculpted eyelids were all demurely closed, though, rather than staring out with the medical-grade glass prosthetics of the most expensive models.

The not-quite-human figures made Fallowfield's back prickle; each had been laid open at the womb and one breast to reveal changes from puberty and childbearing. The closed eyes, flushed cheeks, revealing poses, and sensually painted mouths spoke of an intimate, inviting shame. The curled infant and young woman heavy with the late stage of her first pregnancy didn't trouble him as much as the child and adolescent. The pubescent girl's hand rested on her turned and lowered head like an odalisque to reveal the emerging down in her armpit. Fallowfield's body stirred and he looked away.

The closed, averted eyes and pale, opalescent skin were too much like Sybille, and the dainty child with her arms folded reminded him of Rowena, although without the vitiligo. Both girls were non-verbal and rarely made eye contact, but their attitudes had turned out to be very different. Fallowfield once gave a thought to grooming Rowena to replace Sybille when she aged out of his affections, but he'd quickly learned headstrong Rowena had a fierce temper. Something in him feared the wax girl would growl if he tried to touch her.

Again, Fallowfield glided without consciously directing himself to do so, this time to the locked bookcase, and watched as his hand raised a key to open it. The sweet scent of rag paper and old leather rushed out. The row of ancient spines imprinted in gold invited the brush of his fingertips. He paused at one whose binding seemed extraordinarily fine.

SEVERUS PINAEUS
AMSTELDAMI
1663

His hands shook slightly as he eased the book off the shelf and turned to the title page, illustrated with an engraving of the goddess Diana and her nymphs startled while bathing by the hunter Actaeon; in the background, her hounds ripped apart a stag.

*De **integritatis** et **corruptionis virginum notis**: de graviditate et partu naturali mulierum*

On the front flyleaf was a handwritten note in French.

Ce curieux petit livre sur la Virginité et les fonctions génératrices féminines me paraissant mériter une reliure congruente au sujet est revêtu d'un morceau de peau de femme tanné par moi-même avec du sumac. Dr L. Bouland

[This curious little book on virginity and the generative feminine functions seemed to me to merit a binding pertinent to the subject. It is bound with a piece of female skin, tanned by myself with sumac. Dr L. Bouland]

It wasn't uncommon for fine medical texts to be bound in human skin in earlier centuries, as if to give them greater authority; still, it was strange to hold as it fell open in his cupped palm. Fallowfield paused at an oddly stilted illustration of fetuses that looked like shrunken adults with balloon heads. He had a vertiginous sense of falling into the page. He told himself to put the treatise safely back on the shelf until he was calmer.

Another volume caught his eye. This one had a plain cloth cover and simple title page.

THE
STORY OF MY LIFE.
By
J. MARION SIMS, M.D., LL., D.
Edited by his Son
H. MARION-SIMS, M.D.
1884

Sims had been seen as a giant in his field until political correctness poisoned his reputation. The female slaves on whom Sims experimented were fully conscious while he performed surgery on their genitals, but anesthesia was a recent development at the time, and it was believed by the best minds of the era that Negros felt little pain. Sims asserted that the women were grateful for his attempts to cure them, and indeed he had gone on to be considered the father of modern gynecology.

Fallowfield had read the autobiography in reprint, and opened the book only to check for inscriptions or inserts. As he did, he heard the whispering noise that had bothered him all that day. He shook his head and the sound stopped, but he looked no farther inside.

A pair of heftier, somewhat older tomes drew his attention next.

PRÉCIS
ÉLEMENTAIRE
de
PHYSIOLOGIE
PAR F. MAGENDIE

Docteur en Médecine de la Faculté de Paris; Professeur d'Anatomie, de Physiologie et de Sémiotique; Membre des Sociétés Philomatiqeu et Médicale d'émulation; Associé de la Société de Médecine de Stockholm, etc.

The two volumes had leather spines and thick cardstock covers—probably residents of a working physician's office before ending up in this collection. Darwin, Thomas Huxley, and Bram Stoker had all condemned Magendie for his insistence on dissecting living specimens, yet his pioneering work in physiology had ensured his legacy as a man of science.

Magendie had been insistent that only living, reactive systems could reveal the secrets of their existence, and his discoveries had proved his argument. Rumors that, in his quest for scientific accuracy, he sought subjects for his research not only among the lesser animals but also the mentally unfit denizens of asylums were never proven.

The volume Fallowfield held fell open to a page marked with a folded broadside sheet. The sheet opened up of its own accord to display the text of a speech by the Irish MP who'd drafted Britain's first animal cruelty legislation. In it, the MP called Magendie a disgrace to society, describing one of the physiologist's public vivisections in which a dog had been nailed down by the ears and paws as its facial nerves were dissected, and the animal left overnight and re-examined in the morning to observe the deterioration.

Fallowfield told himself he needed to attend to what he'd come for, and if he ever had the opportunity, he'd revisit the library another time. He strode toward the file cabinet. Again, it seemed a long distance to reach what he aimed for, the pattern in the Oriental rug repeating countless times before he touched the brass handle. The moon had disappeared, leaving only sheets of freezing rain, louder and more insistent, outside the window.

Fallowfield pulled the drawer handle, but it didn't budge. He pulled again more sharply. Adrenaline made him strong enough to rock the heavy cabinet from side to side, clanging each time it hit the floor, but to no effect; the drawers were locked. He ran to the desk, hoping the key might be inside, but that drawer was locked as well. He searched himself for the one he'd used to get to the books. It had vanished.

No paperclips or letter openers he could use as a pick were to be found, but a tooled silver fountain pen he hadn't seen before lay on the blotter. It was engraved with a medical cross on a shield with the subscript *Taconic State Hospital.* He disassembled it, looking for parts that might fit in the cabinet lock. Pitch-black ink began leaking on his fingers. He forced the fill lever back and twisted it from the barrel, flooding ink on the desk and his hands.

Rushing back to the cabinet, he dripped ink on the carpet. It smeared as he tried to work the pen lever into the keyhole, making his fingers too slippery to grip with enough precision. He wiped his palm on his trousers, but the stuff wouldn't dry off. It blended with nervous sweat to leave his hands slick, black, and useless.

Something moved in the display case. Fallowfield turned to see the linen drape on the oldest figure had dropped, leaving the crone and her sexualized wounds uncovered. He suppressed a gag as her glass eyes opened.

She stepped stiffly out of the case and extended something in her wrinkled palm. "Want this?" It was a key.

Fallowfield grabbed for it, black liquid running down his forearms.

The crone shut her hand and stepped back, chuckling. She spoke in a little girl's synthetic voice without moving her mouth, so she laughed and formed words at the same time. "Didn't say you could have it. Ink-and-paper, ink-and-paper, what a mess you've made."

Lunging forward, Fallowfield grabbed her wrist. Her wax flesh was frigid. She slid out of his grip, but came away with none of the black that coated his arms. Where he'd touched her, the liquid turned to obsidian ice crystals on his hand. Her skin was mottled, not just with age, but with a blotchy pattern, raggedly unpigmented on her hands and feet and down the middle of her face. Her wounds wept a cold, thin stream of red she seemed indifferent to.

Fallowfield rasped, "What the hell are you?"

The crone grinned and spoke in the same mechanical voice. "Not Ligeia, that's for sure. You did your best to fill me up with someone else, but it didn't work."

"Rowena? No, she was a child when she died, not—not...this."

"Stupid man. I have hell to pay now. They don't approve of suicide. My punishment is to experience what I could have become if I hadn't given up. I'm serving my time on work release, but that's another story. Anyway, shall we open your file cabinet?"

Fallowfield stepped aside, and the crone hobbled to the lock. She opened the drawer that held his laptop. He pushed in to snatch it, and she held his arm, looking at him sidelong. Her grip froze his tissue to the bone. A sob came out of him, in spite of his hating to give her that much of his weakness.

Rowena licked her motionless lips. "Quiet hands, Hammie. Apologize for being rude and grabby."

"I'll show you rude and grabby, you hideous sow." Wrenching himself around so he could reach with his free hand, he plunged his fingers into the incision in her shriveled womb. She laughed and spat in his face. The spittle burned like dry ice, and his fingers inside her jolted with electric shock. He pulled his hand back, feeling the damage under the black coating.

She let him go, watching him huddle against the wall. Her voice was a chorus of whispers from the center of her slashed, withered chest. "Autistics don't feel, remember? I am Legion, for we are many. You've cast us out, O mighty miracle worker. Fuck you. Let's see what all is in this drawer you're so antsy about. Your protocols define that as obsessive perseveration, you know. I'll have to give you a negative reinforcement."

Fallowfield raised his hands over his face and stammered.

"Use your words, Hammie! I said quiet hands, didn't I?" She spat her venom again, and his shoulder seared.

Obsidian crystals crept up his arms. If they reached his lungs, he'd suffocate. Or would they stop his heart? He struggled to think. Volcanic glass, that's what it was. Black, frozen fire. He needed to please her/them somehow, get her to stop.

"I'm sorry. I'm sorry, Rowena. You know I—"

"Shut up! Yes, I do know you, with your pedophile's Alice carnival and your court of enablers. You've declared that we look human, but we're really not. You get paid to make us the best puppets we can be. You put your hand inside us and make us flap our jaws and move our eyes so you or anyone else can have your precious contact as you please. Go to Hell."

The room turned ashen. The desk, books, and showcase vanished. The carpet was a moldering patch on the floor stained from the leaking roof. The waning moon hung at the same point above the horizon. The frozen rain had turned to silence.

Fallowfield's heart leapt, thinking he was alone, but that was a mistake.

The ice storm roared out of her. "Stay in your seat, Hammie! Your session isn't over."

His teeth chattered. He sat up straight with his back against the foul, crumbling plaster.

Rowena lifted a thick folder from the cabinet, set it where the desk had been, and spread the contents out. The papers stayed suspended in space as if supported from another dimension.

She hefted a subfolder. "So this will be where we learn your sentence, but first, let's have a look at the supporting materials... Okay, the behaviorist Mt. Rushmore—you got your Baron-Cohen, you got your Lovaas, you got your Skinner and Matthew Israel..."

Shuffling the papers, she hummed, harmonizing with herself. Her wounds seemed to be closing, and her vitiligo was more pronounced, its darker areas almost golden. "So, let's make your case. Skinner says all your subjects are black boxes—that is, you can never know what's inside of them. You can only alter their behavior through punishment and reward—"

She picked up a photograph from the pile. "You're being such a good boy, so quiet. Here. Have a Lolita pic. You can look at it for three minutes. That's how you do the rewards, right? Find something precious to the subject, then control his access to it."

Fallowfield hesitated, but reached for the proffered photograph. He regretted his choice; the image was a still from a surveillance video of a screaming child face down in four-point restraints receiving a chlorine dioxide enema. It was from a colleague who specialized in experimental medical treatments for autism. He'd reciprocated with a similar item of Sybille being held down during a shock protocol. The two doctors traded both therapy videos and patients. He waited for Rowena's scorching ice.

Instead, she was calm. "Look at it, Hammie. Full three minutes. Hold it up and do not move your eyes. I'll hold back the crystalizing if you complete the task."

From the edge of his vision, Fallowfield saw Rowena growing. She seemed even more ancient, but her hunched body loomed over him. He held the picture up with his stiffening arm and stared until his eyes watered while she went through the folders, chattering in several voices.

"Oh, here's a good one. Interview with Lovaas, father of applied behavior analysis, as well as conversion therapy for sissy boys. Sweet man. Loved aversives. Nothing like a little torture to get your point across—like the disciple Matthew Israel said about those shock harnesses you use— 'the transformative potential' of pain."

Rowena hummed, mumbling in her whispers, reading from the clipping. "'Autistic children are severely disturbed. People seem to be no more than objects to them... Sometimes parents think the child is visually impaired...because they don't look into your eyes. Many of these kids do not have speech... Some of them have echolalic speech; that is, they simply repeat what you say to them... You have a person in the physical sense—they have hair, a nose, and a mouth—but they are not people in the psychological sense. One way to look at the job of helping autistic kids is to see it as a matter of constructing a person.'"

Fallowfield felt her watching him with her unblinking glass eyes. He struggled to stay motionless. The echoes and whispers in her voice pulled together like a single ancient bell a long way off.

She crouched and laid her frigid hand on his face. "Is that the way you looked at me, Hammie? Looked at my friends? Does poor Miles look like that to you? We watched you hurt him tonight. Did you project that filth into us like that, Hammie? And then train everyone else to see us that way? Because that's really rude. And you're flinching from my touch and you won't look at me. I think I need to extend your keeping-still time."

"Please... I'll do better..."

She went back to the folder, pulling out a slim paperback tucked inside. "Ah, the distinguished Dr. Simon Baron-Cohen FBA FBPsS, born 1958, British clinical psychologist and professor of developmental psychopathology at the University of Cambridge, director of the university's Autism Research Centre and Fellow of Trinity College."

She flipped the book over. *"Mindblindness: An Essay on Autism and Theory of Mind*...MIT Press. I remember this from when I went to the college I never lived to see. The good doctor Baron-Cohen never asked us what we felt, even though AAC was around to give us voices. He'd rather have one of his protégés tell our parents what we must be feeling."

She leafed through the book. "Here it is. 'At the top of my field of vision is the blurry edge of a nose, in front are waving hands... Around me, bags of skin are draped over chairs, and stuffed into pieces of cloth, they shift and protrude in unexpected ways... Imagine that these noisy skin bags suddenly moved toward you, and their noises grew loud, and you had no idea why, no way of explaining them or predicting what they would do next.' Lovely images. It was wonderful when your therapists treated me as though that was what I saw when I looked at them. Have you taken a moment to wonder why I let myself die?"

Rowena was, herself, alone. The clustered revenants of the institution's intentional and collateral sacrifices were a rapt audience in place to offer a supporting chorus.

Shaking from holding the picture up, Fallowfield kept his voice low and cautious. "I've made mistakes. I understand that now."

"Oh, you haven't started to understand all the mistakes you've made, Hammie. Wake up. After you, the deluge. Look at the moon—no, that doesn't mean you can put that picture down—see, it hasn't moved. Do you comprehend the implications?"

Fallowfield's eyes widened.

Rowena cupped her fingers as if to cradle the lopsided sphere outside the window. "This thing you do to us, Hammie, you know we blow the suicide risk assessment scores out the roof after we've been through it, and yet you do everything you can to make sure no one listens when we try to say what's killing us. Think about it, Hammie. I have all the time in the universe, right here in my hand."

The waning moon crawled into her palm like a trusting pet. "Should I open the laptop, or shall we stipulate I know what's in it? What is it with guys like you needing to record yourselves with your coups, anyway? You couldn't just erase that feed? It'd look bad it was missing, but you'd blame someone else."

A shadow of a defiant laugh flickered on Fallowfield's face. "She's beautiful, isn't she? You can never have that first time again."

Rowena loomed over him and spat on his ankle. He felt the jolt, but his body below the neck was paralyzed. He set his jaw against the pain.

The voice coming out of the hag jeered and moaned like a distant flock of crows. "That one was for Miles, but this is about Sybille. She's had every molecule of self-determination stripped out of her, deliberately. Can you imagine how time crawls for her? Brainwashed forty hours a week from the age of three. Put this thing on, obey that person, stand under those lights, once Mommy figured out she could monetize those weird looks. When did the child learn how to refuse anything? What a conquest. Bleach purges and hyperbaric chamber treatments to cure her, how could she know what hurt her anymore?"

Listening for his own heartbeat, Fallowfield realized his involuntary life functions were closing down. Every time he breathed in, another surge of obsidian spread through him. "What do you want, Rowena?"

She seemed transfixed by the softly glowing orb she held. After an eternity, she spoke to it in a single childish, synthesized voice. "No cameras caught me. How could that be? I went from the institute to the outside of the old building, and no one saw me. I bother the investigators in their sleep, don't I, sweetie? They wake up with new questions." She smoothed her hand over the moon, not quite touching it, and hummed.

He repeated, with the last of his breath, "What do you want?"

"They tried to find me. It was too late, but they tried."

The obsidian crawled into his veins. Stars began to appear in Rowena's towering form.

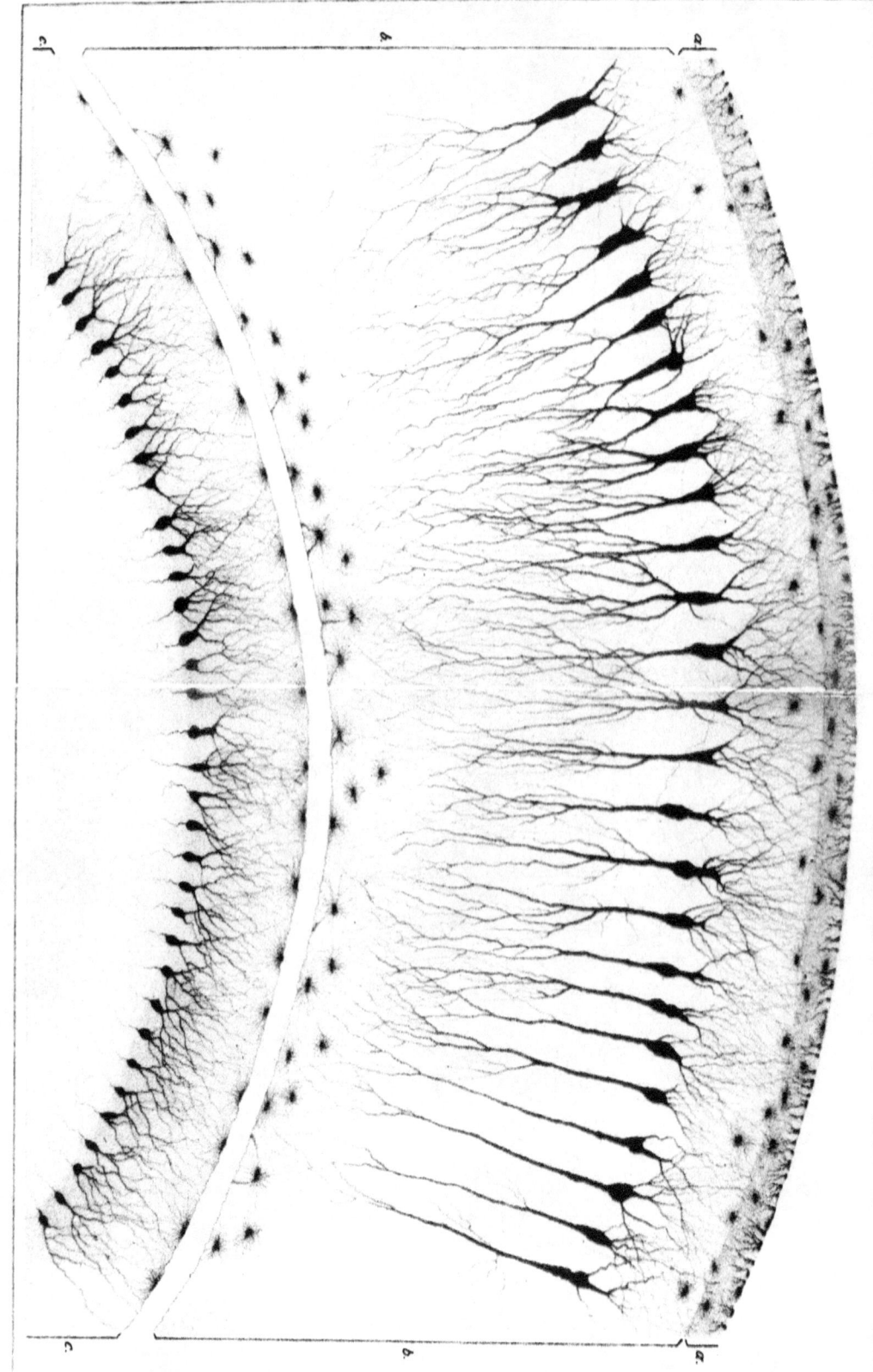

EXTINGUISHING

The bruise across Krysta's shoulder deepened with another slam into the nylon strap. She clamped her mouth shut. It wouldn't help to complain again when her coworker stomped the brakes and threw her against the seatbelt one more time. He was hard to talk to on his good days.

She rubbed her clavicle. On the rural highway, there wasn't reliable cellphone coverage for calling a friend to pass the time. Thirty-eight teeth-grinding miles of dead air each way; twenty-five down, thirteen left before she could sink into bed.

The pallid sun had gone down long ago, and a heavy, rising moon glimmered intermittently between clouds full of some kind of disagreeable precipitation that hadn't yet firmly decided what kind of frozen slop to be.

No point stewing in regrets.

The enchantment of the Civil War-era farmhouse where she rented two rooms with kitchen and clawfoot tub privileges was long gone. When she accepted CareWell Institute's offer as a pediatric behavioral health technician, Krysta's parents wanted to pay the difference for an overpriced apartment within walking distance. Instead, for most of the last year, she'd driven the mile to and from the orderly's old trailer to carpool. Working hours demanded leaving and returning in the dark. The spectacular Taconic Mountain view she passed was nothing but black space except on the longest summer days.

She'd avoided facing Upstate New York snow behind the wheel until Brian's recent week off to stalk whitetails. It had gone badly enough, she'd been happy to see him on his first day back. The feeling faded quickly.

In the close quarters of the pickup cab, the change in Brian was glaring. His good ol' boy physique had shrunk, his clothes loose and his cheeks gaunt. He hadn't spoken since she got in the truck in the fading light of an hour ago.

Krysta searched for an icebreaker. Speculation on what had happened to the CareWell Institute's director was endemic at work.

"Do you think we'll ever find out what happened to Dr. Fallowfield?"

"Not likely."

Rubbery chatter of wipers on the slushy windshield.

Playing with her hair, she tried again. "So, will Dr. Pratt or Kelli Rivers take over the institute, or do you think the board will bring in someone else?" She favored motherly Agnes Pratt, with her plain, plus-sized suits, church-lady makeup, and home-dyed hair. Realistically, Fallowfield's sleek, gym-rat protégé Kelli would be taking charge.

Brian stared at the road. "Haven't the faintest."

As they'd left the grounds, she'd noticed a sheriff's department vehicle parked by one of the Victorian edifices now used as storage for outdated records and office furniture.

"I'll bet you know about those buildings Fallowfield was digging around in before he disappeared. That's where that runaway died too, huh? The one with the skin condition? I heard none of the cameras picked her up."

"Ask McCoy. He knows more than I do."

The McCoy farm was up from Brian's trailer on Abenaki Ridge. Morningstar McCoy was Krysta's landlord, an aging hippie and amateur local historian with a prized collection of documents and artifacts. A root canal was preferable to accepting his offer to show her the musty things.

Brian had been close to the client who'd died of exposure right before he'd left for his hunting. She'd escaped the CareWell facility somehow, fallen asleep against the granite foundation of the old main building, and succumbed to the frigid mountain wind sometime in the night. No one had been held responsible for her elopement.

Staring at the dead CD player, Krysta listened to the tires kicking slush into the wheel wells.

Closed up in a barrel with a zombie that's lost his appetite.

The institute's hardline behaviorist doctrine had seemed like the rigorous mindset she needed. Train autistic clients to be indistinguishable from their neurotypical peers. No self-soothing stims, rocking, fidgeting, hand-flapping, and mindless mumbling. No tolerance for sensitivities to innocuous stimuli.

Subjects are black boxes. No speculating on what might be inside. Responding to client outbursts rewards undesirable conduct; don't consider what caused the distress. Define negative behaviors and develop programs to extinguish them.

Clean, simple, and effective.

Lately, Krysta found it harder. One child had a cracked tooth. After acting out for a week, he was taken to an independent medical clinic. There, he was permitted to use his communication tablet, and the problem was found.

Clients were to use proper speech within the institute. If they couldn't verbalize their problems, it would motivate them to try harder. Autistic muteness might be based in profound uncoordination between brain and body, but urgency would encourage the breakthrough necessary to overcome it. Krysta had seen for herself that sometimes so-called nonverbal children could muster a few words when they wanted to desperately enough.

"I wonder if Miles is doing better on the new protocol. Dr. Pratt says he isn't misbehaving as much." Krysta was more talking to herself than asking. "I hardly see him anymore, but he did speak a little in the last session I had with him."

Brian turned and glared. "You know damned well I've got nothing to say about that."

Krysta tugged harder on her hair. Miles had recently been prescribed a locked harness that delivered painful electric shocks to control his escalating noncompliance. He'd been scrambling onto cabinets and even ductwork. Closets and lockers had to be double-secured from his clever fingers, and he was fond of disconnecting surveillance electronics. After the harness, he'd begun self-harming sometimes, but at least they'd been able to control him.

Autistics were usually clumsy, but sometimes had singular physical skills, and Miles's was climbing. Once, Dr. Pratt had to give him a happy shot to get him down. The institute prided itself on not using chemical straitjackets, but Agnes Pratt quietly did the kinder, necessary things, and the drug cabinet in her office was well known among the staff.

Just past the intersection of the state route and Abenaki Ridge Road, Brian braked and downshifted the venerable manual transmission, engaging the four-wheel drive. Even at ten miles an hour, the deceleration was too sudden.

The pickup fishtailed on black ice. The focus of its headlights swung away from a ditch and decaying split rail fence in a leftward skid, flooded a driveway festooned with Christmas decorations, swept back across the narrow road, and came to rest pushing into the looming woods. Brian worked the clutch and coaxed the truck back to its lugubrious trek.

A lame, dark-coated coywolf crossed their path toward the trees at the outer reach of the light beams. Appearing mostly wolf by size, its long, canny face and lanky build showed the coyote in its genes. Coyotes had bred with the original wolves of the region, and though settler humans had exterminated those first canine inhabitants of the mountain forests, their blood lived on in the crafty mix that knew the killing ways of non-indigenous people and how to survive them.

The way the truck was crawling, the mongrel animal could have crossed without them slowing at all.

Then Brian started mumbling, and they coasted to a stop.

"Brian? Are you okay?"

Sweat gleamed on his face, and his lips moved.

She felt a tug on her arm. Brian turned toward her, his features caught in the sleet-scattered glow coming in the windshield. The wipers cut arcs in accumulating slush, casting moving shadows on his face. His pupils were so dilated, his light blue eyes looked black as he stared at the empty space beside her.

The tug came again. Brian fixated on the arm of her puffer jacket where the thing pulling at her would be, but the quilting was uncompressed. Krysta felt her back prickle.

"I...can't take you home anymore." He eased the clutch in, and the truck began creeping forward. "You'll need to find another way."

* * *

If Krysta was bothered by wind leaking around the rippled hand-poured windowpanes in her rooms, it was up to her to deal with it. She'd scraped flaking paint off the sashes and put up plastic sheeting with duct tape, but nothing stayed stuck to the splintering wood that smelled of hidden rot deep in the walls.

She bundled the fallen poly and tossed the wad in her bedroom corner.

Just the cap on a perfectly lovely evening.

The rest of the dead-silent ride back had been a bad *Twilight Zone* rerun. When she'd gone inside Brian's trailer for a broom to clear her car, she'd startled his deaf cat and it clawed her. Now the red stripes across her hand were getting inflamed.

Her landlord and his wife laughed downstairs by the massive enameled stove. From her doorway, she watched Lucinda McCoy's slim, strong back and thick braid as she cooked. Then her landlady looked up, her expression slyly amused. Krysta turned away from the glow of the steam-fogged kitchen, closed her door, and shoved her goosebumped limbs into the flannel pajamas she'd left warming on the radiator.

Morn McCoy's family had owned the homestead forever, and his arm was crippled from a farm accident. That was more than enough to know about him. Neither tall, sinewy spouse was stooped, though their hair was graying. They'd waved her over to join them when she'd come in, but she didn't eat their kind of food and they knew it. Cindy had stood over the pot, tasting and adjusting, ladling in home-canned tomatoes, pepper sauce, and dried herbs from her garden, brushing a steam-loosened curl from her forehead. Now the scent of short ribs elicited a mouthwatering pang. Krysta yanked the covers back and crawled into bed.

The sheets were frigid, the bedsprings poked, and the delicious smell teased. Krysta had been faithfully vegan for nine months. To keep her resolve, she pictured a strand from Morn's blackish beard in the cooking. He was always using his chin to lever things. Maybe he couldn't reach to clean himself properly because of his arm, but he didn't wash much or use deodorant. She couldn't picture what Cindy found attractive in him.

Downstairs, Morn said it was time to check on the kids, a joke about the goats. There were no children. The rickety door closed after the pair.

Krysta put on her robe and headed downstairs. Morn took several hours for evening chores. Sometimes while he was out, when the dishes were done, Cindy made tea while Krysta vented about work. Cindy didn't say much, but she was often uncomfortably on point when she did.

After putting prepackaged meatless minestrone into her microwave, Krysta peeked into the evergreen-scented shadows of the parlor. The Christmas tree was garlanded with popcorn and topped by a string-wrapped husk angel with a dried-apple head and corn silk hair. Its mummified rooster wings unfurled darkly iridescent; they'd been positioned to stiffen in place, nailed to a barn rafter all autumn. Fir boughs wound with bittersweet topped the doorways, the bright, poisonous berries up out of the way of the half-wild cats that kept mice out of the house. The fireplace was cold and smelled of ashes. An uneasy sense that she didn't belong in the quiet room kept her from exploring further.

There was a weighty thump, and Cindy grunted outside.

Fumbling with the loose doorknob, Krysta called into the night. "Can I help?"

Soft growling abruptly stopped. Another smell—a raw, metallic, salty tang—carried in the chill. Krysta flicked on the yellow outside bulb.

"Damn it!" Cindy's voice had an unfamiliar edge. "Turn that off and get in the house! If I want help I'll ask for it."

Krysta shut the door, dizzy.

The image burned. Large, long-toothed mongrel canines backing away into darkness made more complex by the fall of glistening snow, shreds of moonlight, and the steam of visceral warmth. Scattered animal parts—hooved forelegs severed at the elbow, goat heads with staring eyes and lolling tongues, offal piles smearing the snow—and Cindy snarling, her breath misting, hands darkened in a nameless color distorted by the amber bug light.

Padded footsteps returned.

Cindy called, "Catch!" and then, "That's all, kiddies." Coatless in the doorway, she brushed pinkish snow off herself. "Real life too much for ya, eh, Krys?" She went to the cast-iron sink and washed ruddy smears off her arms. "Open that cabinet next to the fridge and pick your poison."

Krysta gaped.

The overhead light caught Cindy's crow's feet and the gray glinting in the deep auburn at her temples. "Sit down, then. We did the winter butchering. Last year we waited for you to go home for Christmas. You've been around long enough now. We eat the animals we raise. They aren't for decoration. Those mongrel beasts get the scraps—they'd dig everything up if we buried it anyway. Morn can't abide dogs, and the pack keeps intruders away." She wiped her hands, crossed the kitchen, and pulled out a bottle of bourbon.

Krysta did as she was told. "Why...doesn't he like...like dogs?" That was supposed to be a bad sign, people who didn't like dogs.

Cindy half-filled two juice glasses with whiskey. "Because they're suck-ups." She took a solid sip. "Bred to serve and please."

"The big black one with the limp..." Krysta trailed off.

"Oh, that one. You could say he looks after things around here. If you saw him, he wanted to be seen."

The golden liquid burned. The scent of fir slipped in underneath the intoxicating concoction on the stove. With a pang, Krysta realized her landlady's green eyes were beautiful, like an ache that had just broken the surface from a long way down.

Cindy leaned in, the heat of her body inside her blood-flecked work clothes palpable. "Our kind mates for life, but we do as we will. I can show you things. You've been watching. You don't have to be shy, but it's fine if you are. There's all the time in the turning stars to make up your mind."

She pulled at Krysta's fingers gently. "What happened to your hand? Our cats wouldn't let you close enough to get clawed so deep."

Tears started as Krysta disgorged how everything turned strange and Brian freaked and had left her stuck without a ride. She let go of Cindy's pass at her as a processing error somewhere in the boozy exchange.

Her face hardening, Cindy pushed her chair back. "Losing that girl hit Brian like a sledgehammer, Krysta. He comes back from the service, thinks working with autistic kids will be kinder—finds himself complicit in damaging them. He actually thinks about shit like human dignity and personal responsibility. Cut him some slack."

Krysta tried to catch her sniffles before they got ugly. "Do...do you think he might be obsessing—like to the point of hallucinating?" Suggestible people could be affected by the delusions of others. It wasn't nice to think of herself that way, but at least it meant the world was more or less normal.

Cindy shrugged and topped up their drinks. "Morn has to go into town tomorrow. You can ride with him. Probably later than your regular time. You can call your supervisor once you're on 87. Snow's supposed to clear up by noon. I'll drive your car in then and leave it in the lot."

Krysta rubbed her face, tried to think of words.

"You don't imbibe much, do you? You could say 'thank you' and it wouldn't hurt my feelings."

The room wobbled on an axis Krysta couldn't pin down. The delectable smell from the covered pot overwhelmed the thinner one of her cooling microwaved soup.

"When was the last time you ate?" Cindy lifted the lid and stirred. "Come over here. Then we'll deal with your hand."

Beckoning, Cindy's eyes flickered deep emerald.

Krysta noticed red under Cindy's nails as she picked up a knife, lifted a steaming rib from the thick, savory liquid with the point, and deftly stripped the flesh before dropping the bone back in.

She cupped Krysta's jaw in her firm, callused palm. "Open."

Obediently, Krysta closed her eyes and allowed Cindy to slide the pinch of tender, spicy meat into her mouth.

"Good girl. It's chevon. You like it, don't you?"

A moan slipped from Krysta's throat as she suckled the long, weather-hardened fingers, her body inviting the other hand as it slithered into her robe and down her abdomen inside her waistband. Then the fingers she ached for slid away.

Cindy laughed, flashing bright teeth, and reached under the sink for a brown bottle. "Slow down, little lady. Let's see what kitty did to you."

She took Krysta's injured hand, kissed the feverish punctures, and held her wrist firmly as she poured peroxide into the tiny wounds.

Krysta winced and gasped, trying to conceal the shudder that started deep in her belly.

"You savor the pain too. I enjoy that in a girl."

* * *

Now, hours later, Krysta was by her bedroom window as the lame coywolf stood quietly in the field below, and another, smaller one with a paler coat snatched a bloody thing from his mouth. It galloped around him, circling widdershins, shaking its head, feinting and lunging. The setting moon hung full and huge, scraping the mountain horizon, unscreened by the earlier storm clouds.

A wash of solstice green and red, evergreen and emerald, bitter berries and dripping sanguine, flooded through her. She felt herself dropping down on all fours, drawn into the game between them. She fought to pull herself back up behind the glass.

A young girl with a sickly luminescence bowed rhythmically, her arms around herself, watching the animals. She glanced up, catching

Krysta's gaze with black, bottomless eyes. Krysta struggled to get free as something dragged her by the arm. The spinning ground came closer and then became cavernous. Battling vertigo, she found herself snarled in bedsheets on the inhospitable mattress.

* * *

Next morning, Krysta hunched against the passenger door, avoiding Morn's teasing.

"I come from Albany." She pulled her turtleneck up higher, staring at the fogged window by her face. "The monsters I knew wore suits and haunted marble hallways."

Morn grinned. "Nevertheless, you walk among monsters now."

The world outside the battered Jeep was a swirl of white. Travel meant squinting a half-dozen car lengths ahead and guessing. The Jeep's low beams created a glimmering wall a few feet beyond the hood.

Krysta hung onto the armrest. "What monsters?"

The heater diffused Morn's stink into every crevice. A slow grin started on his lips. "Now that Cin's touched you, that should change—and it's no threat to me. She does what she likes and so do I."

A fierce flush bloomed fire in Krysta's cheeks and her lips welded together.

"Monsters are metaphors with substance." Morn indicated his mutilated arm with his chin.

"I think of monsters as people like Jeffrey Epstein." Krysta's throat was tight, but she wasn't giving ground. "How is he a metaphor?"

"The Big Bad Wolf? Epstein's just this year's mask for him—let's try something harder. How about those kids you work on?"

"What are you talking about? They're sweet, not monsters. They smile when I come in."

"Fear can wear a smile. Not them I'm speaking of. Your masters draw up the strategy. You devise the tactics. All very scientific. Do you chart how many times higher the suicide rate is for survivors of compliance training? It's about ninefold, if memory serves."

Krysta considered demanding to be let out, but they were twenty miles from town. "What do you know about my job anyway?"

Morn's jaw muscles bulged. "I know its roots feed on the suffering soaking the ground under those buildings. The job always claims to help its victims and silences anyone who survives its kindness."

Cool rage stiffened Krysta's spine. "Don't worry about me coming back tonight. I'll get a hotel room."

"Cindy will pack your things. Not like we didn't try to show you." Morn clicked his teeth. "Your runaways have found sanctuary at the house on the ridge for generations, back to the little savages punished for speaking Anishinaabemowin instead of proper English—sound familiar? 'Kill the Indian and Save the Man,' right? Was the least my family could do, sheltering them, considering it was their land to begin with."

"As usual, I have no idea what you're talking about." After she said that, the memory of Brian telling her to ask Morn about the history of the institute flashed through her mind.

Too late now.

"Residential school. Native kids—gotta make them indistinguishable from their peers—except the master gets to define what a peer is. Always control and compliance. Hardheaded women sent to rot in the state asylum for daring think for themselves..." Morn eyed Krysta's body pointedly, "...or desiring other women. Abenaki Ridge was the first stop on their freedom train. Read some history. Look for the central utility tunnel access behind the control room in the arcade. Connects all the buildings on the grounds. Fallowfield killed the cameras covering it, and he hasn't been around to switch them back on. Maybe something he did caught up with him."

Krysta turned away.

"But you're different, of course." Attending to the steering, Morn's tone softened. "Just like everyone else who's ever worked there."

* * *

"Dr. Pratt?" Krysta hurried to catch up to the matronly march of her white-coated supervisor. "Could I talk to you a moment?"

"Certainly, Krysta. I've been worrying. Brian hasn't appeared yet. And what happened to your poor hand?" Agnes Pratt eased the conversation into the ladies' room alcove.

Dabbing her eyes, Krysta brushed off the question about her hand and described Morn's insults on the ride in.

Dr. Pratt nodded. "Of course you can't go back, dear. Perfectly understandable."

Krysta explained the budget hotel was full of skiers and the bed-and-breakfast too expensive.

"I was wondering..." Krysta lowered her eyes, "...if it would be, um, permissible if I slept in my office...until I find something? While I'm here, I could chart out the backlog of restraint and seclusion files for the Department of Education report."

The institute had a higher rate of deaths than similar facilities, and had been repeatedly cited for poor recordkeeping.

"I can review the raw video and generate the paperwork." Krysta glanced up. "This bureaucratic stuff has to be a massive extra burden for you without Dr. Fallowfield."

"That's a generous offer, but these are highly confidential materials. It *is* a staggering amount of work. Let me give it—"

A wail and crash came from a classroom.

Dr. Pratt rushed toward the sound. "Grab a papoose board! Six-to-twelve size," she called over her shoulder.

Pulling her key lanyard over her head as she ran, Krysta turned down an unlit side hall to the row of timeout booths—padded, windowless, cinderblock-partitioned cubicles. In a nod to contemporary practices, they were open at the top to the steel trusses and ductwork of the roof systems to relieve claustrophobia. One was used to store restraint equipment.

A child's screams and several octaves of adult yelling echoed behind her.

The papoose board was a tough, coffin-shaped, body-length plastic plank. Three large, blue, velcroed nylon petals ran down each side. It bore a logo of a smiling, pink-skinned toddler wearing an ersatz Native American headdress. The cartoon child was loosely restrained by a strap around its middle, its hands and feet free, a usage directly contradicted by the businesslike instruction diagram underneath it. Three each of four sizes, infant to adult, leaned against the cinderblock.

A whimper came from the adjoining room. The corridor was empty. Hallway-mounted screens for the motion-activated cameras inside the cubicles were dark except for the one her movements had awakened. She looked down at the top of her own head, then turned as something moved in the corner.

It skittered behind a stack of accessories—head and arm immobilizers, spit hoods and anti-scratch sleeves in plastic boxes, loops of nylon strapping hung on wall-hooks. It seemed almost too big for whatever kind of rodent it probably was, and that somehow it should have moved the stuff along the wall trying to get all of itself in behind. There was the soft but unmistakable sound of a mournful animal's voice. Perhaps someone had brought a pet to work for some kind of therapy thing and it had slipped away and gotten lost. Even if the creature wasn't a rat, after her run-in with Brian's cat, she wasn't about to reach for it.

Dr. Pratt yelled for the board, and Krysta shut the door.

* * *

Krysta eyed the cot and rubbed her face. Her office overlooked the parking lot. Her car sat lonely under a lamp pole, filled with the few neatly repacked boxes of belongings she'd arrived with at Abenaki Ridge. Glare from the security spotlights slashed across the carpet.

The report was done. Dr. Pratt had given her the password for the records flagged as problematic. The videos were transcribed appropriately and erased. Scans of handwritten logs had internal codes for everything from biting to feces-smearing. Krysta created anodyne summaries before deleting the originals. She checked the bandage on her hand Cindy had wrapped so carefully the night before, yawned, and closed the file.

Bored and conflicted, she clicked through the Taconic Behavioral Health Complex website. Under the *history of the campus* tab were subheadings for the St. Isaac Jogues Boarding School for Indian Youth and the Taconic State Hospital for the Mentally Infirm.

The map placed the residential school in the newer part of the complex, on or near the location of the present institute. Rows of blank-faced, dark-haired children in uniforms sat on the lawn of a sturdy, charmless building. Dignified boys in long braids and tribal clothes morphed into shellshocked versions of Moe from the Three Stooges in ill-fitting suits and hacked haircuts.

That much of Morn McCoy's story was confirmed.

More intriguing were tintypes of Victorian madhouse scenes haunted by hollow-eyed women in white gowns. There was a link to a book with engraved illustrations called *Modern Persecution, Or, Insane Asylums Unveiled.* The author had been committed to an Illinois institution similar to Taconic in the mid-1800s by her tyrannical husband. Krysta lost herself in the dramatic retelling, full of assumed identities and smuggled letters.

* * *

It was after midnight. The heating system roared quietly. Krysta had just finished reading an internal report discussing a pending lawsuit by the mother of a deceased client. It named Dr. Fallowfield as the father of the nonverbal teenager's unborn child. Dr. Pratt had said Dr. Rivers would handle that folder, but Krysta knew how to clear internal histories.

Onscreen, from the same folder, a video-recorded ABA session was about to go bad.

The girl with vitiligo, on the last morning of her life, was starting the third hour of a session scheduled to last the full daytime shift. Krysta fast-forwarded through a ninety-minute contest of wills between the child, named Rowena, and a new therapist. Dr. Pratt supervised without intervening.

The subject is to complete the assigned task, no matter the duration or expressed distress. The therapist cannot relent and thereby reinforce undesirable behavior. Noncompliance must be extinguished.

Rowena was to transfer a hundred pennies spread across the table into a pink plastic piggy bank. She wailed as her clumsy fingers were placed repeatedly over the coins, forced to fumble with them and guided to push them into the slot. A well-worn stuffed toy, a pony or unicorn, was just out of her reach, and she glanced at it obsessively. When she tried to self-soothe by hugging herself and rocking, the toy was put in a latched box out of sight.

The girl was observed impassively by the professionals as she screamed herself to exhaustion and went limp. Her hands were worked puppet-like by the new therapist standing behind her to continue the assignment. She flinched from the reward-tickles and shrieky joy that came with every successful deposit.

Finally, with a few dozen pennies remaining, Rowena exploded, whirling around and smashing the bank to the floor. The pig split in half, its contents spilling onto the linoleum as she flapped her hands.

Dr Pratt stepped forward. "No! Enough. Look. At. Me." She held Rowena's wrists. "Eye contact! Quiet hands!"

Rowena twisted free. She yanked the junior therapist's sleeve. Her albino fingers, marked like they'd been plunged in splashing milk, frantically mimed entering words into a speech-synthesizing AAC tablet.

"NO!" Dr. Pratt took the girl by the shoulders and spun her, their faces almost touching. "No more tablet! You have verbal words. Use them."

Rowena lunged, biting the doctor's nose.

Dr. Pratt pinned the yowling child face-down, her arm twisted behind her. An orderly brought a papoose board. In seconds, Rowena was wrapped like a cocoon. The adults left, Dr. Pratt dabbing a small smear of blood from her face. Rowena's screams gradually abated.

The incident report noted Rowena was given two ounces of water prior to being put in seclusion, at which time Dr. Pratt administered a moderate dose of Midazolam. Response to the sedative was within the expected range.

The next clip was a time-lapse triggered by movement. Except to relieve herself in the corner once, Rowena remained curled on the rubberized floor. Every half-hour, the intercom ordered her to sit up with her back to the wall. Rowena's flinches caused the low-light camera to record for five seconds. She ignored the commands.

"Just a black box," something said in a whisper like seething sleet.

Twisting to look behind her, Krysta saw nothing.

Onscreen, the cubicle door was slightly open, letting in a sliver of light. Rowena raised her head, then bolted from the room.

The third video was pieced from separate feeds. Fallowfield strode through the halls, picked up by each camera in turn. The clip caught Rowena hiding as the doctor stood at the hallway intersection, trailing him when he began walking again, smiling smugly to himself. The two traversed the gaudy reward galleria where clients redeemed good-behavior tokens for trinkets and amusements. Krysta's arm hairs raised as she watched them enter the arcade, slip among the giant fiberglass figures, and disappear into the control room. The video stopped.

That was how Rowena had escaped unseen to lie outside against the cold stone until she froze, in sight of the lights of the new institute. Fallowfield had used the tunnel as he'd clearly done many times, but that night he'd delivered a child to her death alongside him. Someone had let her out of the cubicle, and he was the only one the video showed near it.

Krysta looked out the window. Her car wasn't there. Cindy had left the keys with security. They were now in Krysta's pocket. The light caught snow falling on empty asphalt.

Maintenance must have towed it out of the way to plow the lot.

Her computer screen flickered out, and the lamp died. She peeked into the hall, and blackness.

Then the whimpering.

The sound she'd heard when she'd gotten the papoose board, but now reverberating from below. The vibration echoed in her bones. Clamping her hand over her mouth, she willed the tuning to stop. It receded softly.

Fingers trembling, praying Dr. Pratt was working late, she called from her cellphone.

"What's the matter, dear?"

Words wouldn't come out right, fumbling through the whimpering hum.

"Let me have maintenance check. Hold on, I'll get them...yes...stay on the line, dear...yes." There was background sound. "There's a breaker out in your part of the building. The noises may be a transformer arcing. Why don't you make your way to my office? I'll get you a nice cup of tea started."

The connection cut before Krysta could ask Dr. Pratt to talk her through the length of the north wing, down a flight of stairs, and across the back hall of the main building.

Breathe. Act like a grownup.

The lights had to be on somewhere.

Widely spaced emergency illumination glimmered at floor level. Fingertips running along the wall, she counted doors, but couldn't picture how many should be there. At an intersecting hall, she blanked.

Stairs. Right or ahead?

She opened the flashlight on her phone.

Beyond the beam, something moved. The phone dropped, sliding away on the linoleum. Crawling toward it, she smelled a large animal, felt its heat and breath. Shoved it hard, the coarse fur and massive ribs against her palms. A soft, deep, wounded cry trailed off. The beast vanished. Her phone clattered down, making a distant crack when it hit the bottom of the stairwell two flights below.

Trace the sound.

An emergency light on the landing.

Yes!

Clinging to the welded rail, Krysta reached out her toes for each step. The whimpering reverberated in muffled, overlapping wails. Descent drew her closer to disintegration. Pushing her hand against her lips, her body told her, *No echoes. Don't let it in. No harmonizing.*

The main building was beyond the double doors a half-flight below. A cup of tea waited for her. Shoulders squared, she pushed on. As the doors closed behind her, the wailing subsided.

The main corridor extended ahead. At the far end, ceiling fluorescents and holiday decorations glowed. Rubbery legs wouldn't let Krysta run, but she hurried.

Dr. Pratt's office door was open.

"Hello, Krysta. You've been getting your cardio, I see." Dr. Pratt went to the electric kettle. "I didn't think it was that far a walk. I remember you liking Constant Comment—with honey, right? This isn't genuine Bigelow, I'm afraid, and it may have cooled. Do sit."

Still breathing hard, Krysta collapsed into the offered chair. She'd just closed her eyes when she felt a disembodied tug on her arm. A stifled scream lodged in her throat.

"Dear, you seem very out of sorts." Dr. Pratt stirred the cup and handed it to her.

The orange flavor tasted artificial, the tepid tea so thick with honey it was syrup, but Krysta dutifully sipped it. Dr. Pratt offered to make a new cup; Krysta shook her head and finished. She did feel calmer, but her mouth was cottony and her words still weren't working.

"Better?" Dr. Pratt sat in front of Krysta and stroked her face. "We can never know what's inside another's mind."

Krysta nodded. She wasn't clear on what was in her own mind, let alone someone else's, but Dr. Pratt sounded wise.

"You know, as a supervisor, I can see when any folder is open on another computer. Now, I'd like you to show me where you first heard that sound that troubles you." Dr. Pratt helped her up.

It was such a long walk, and Krysta tried to remember why they were taking it. Dr. Pratt kept asking her gentle questions until she wasn't sure she'd really heard or felt anything. Stumbling as they came on the row of cubicles, Krysta pointed at the one beyond the storage.

"This one?" Dr. Pratt unlocked the door.

Krysta lurched forward, her brain spinning.

Dr. Pratt helped guide her to the floor. "Why don't you lie back, dear..."

Comforting wraps came up around her. Settling into the papoose board, she sighed as Dr. Pratt smoothed the hair away from her face.

"I'm not quite sure how this will go, Krysta." Dr Pratt shifted on her knees. "It was good of that monkey to disconnect the surveillance in here on his current escapade, although I do hope he shows up soon. Heaven knows what the little pest is getting into, but I'm not quite ready to alert security for a search. I haven't yet brought the camera to the attention of maintenance. You'll have your privacy."

All Krysta could manage was a humming noise in her mouth.

"You've had a massive dose of Midazolam, enough to forget everything of today, possibly enough never to remember anything again." Dr. Pratt sighed. "When questions come, I'll indicate you've been troubled, and I've discovered you self-medicating from the cabinet in my office. The hall surveillance will show you describing your hallucinations. The record will confirm that I left you here to calm down and returned to find whatever it is I'll find."

Dr. Pratt checked her watch.

"You were told not to look at that folder." She got up stiffly. "When you did, you left me no other choice." She closed the door.

With nothing else to do, Krysta stared into the reflections and shadows of the rafters. Something long and dark hung like a pendulum, twisting in the currents of warm air.

There used to be a kid who climbed...

* * *

The pair of coywolves snuffled around the little padded room. Miles eased down from the rafter, his body remaining hung by a restraint strap overhead, and wrapped his arms around the big, dark, wolfish one with the limp. The other one, more sleekly built, with an auburn glint to her coat, sniffed at Krysta's bandaged hand under the nylon binding and nuzzled her cooling face.

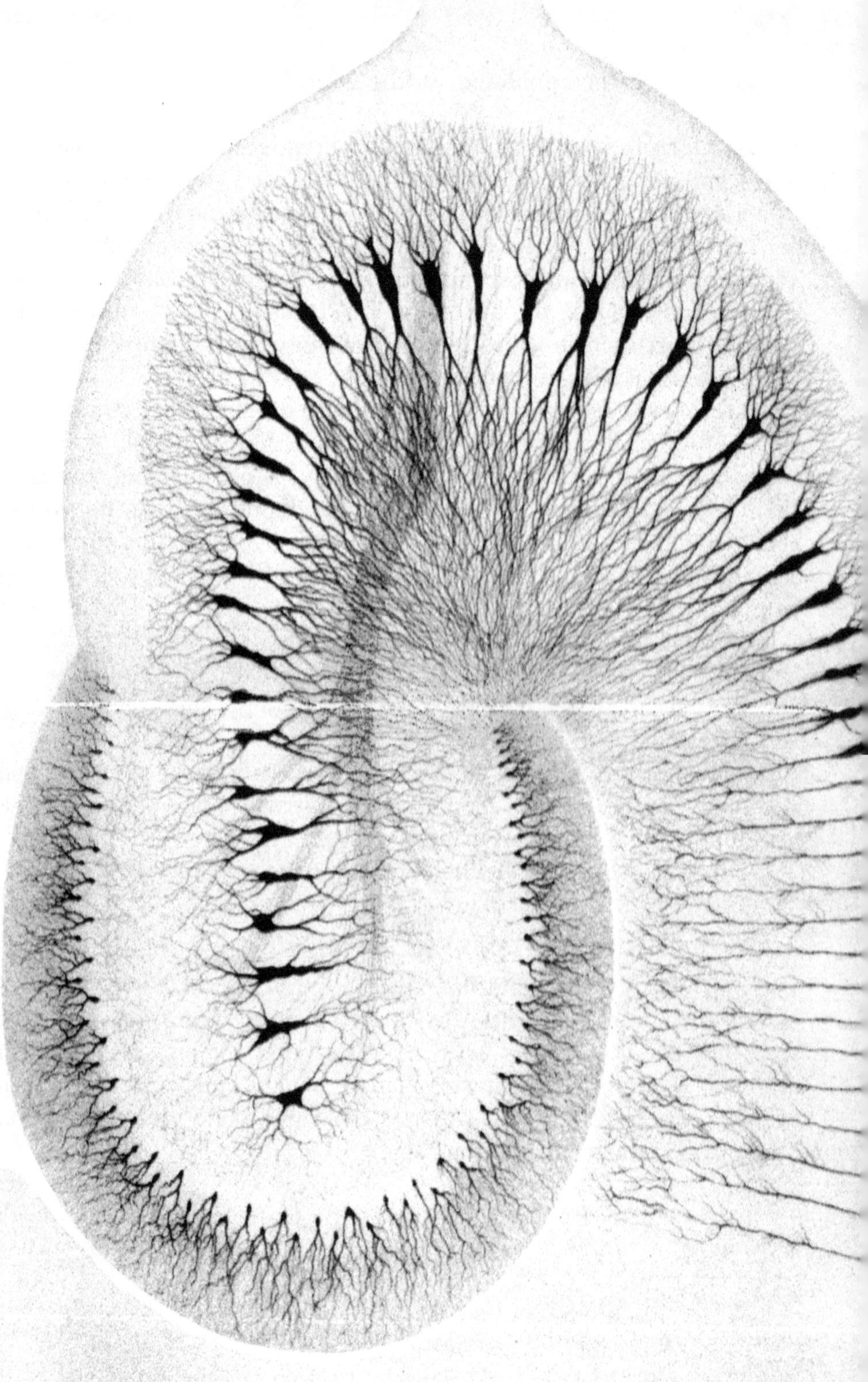

P.A. Ogheri inc.

POLAR DAWN

Sybille sat on the rubber-covered floor, swaying and smiling. The open industrial ceiling above carried echoes of her friend who'd hung himself from one of its trusses after disabling the surveillance camera. She welcomed lingering wisps of him into herself. They would help her find him later. She could smell the shifters who'd come for him after he passed, their earthy canine traces in the blue vinyl padding on the walls.

The intercom said, "Sybille, no rocking, please. Until Dr. Fallowfield says otherwise, no more exceptions for you. Your mother wants you to become a civilized adult. Dr. Rivers agrees it's time to extinguish these attention-seeking behaviors, and she's in charge now. No stimming and no noises for fifteen minutes—then we can let you out."

Sybille imagined sending lightning through the speaker in the timeout room to the staff monitor watching her somewhere in the Panopticon. That's what her sister had called it—the prison of eyes. The last thing she wanted was attention. Even the calming "self-stimulation" of moving her body rhythmically was forbidden. She looked up at the newly repaired camera and gave it a serene, closed-mouthed grin. For her, it was a strong expression. Autism made her baseline countenance an unreadable mask, and that served her purposes.

The intrusion had jolted her out of her meditation as she was gliding into the well. She calculated her not-a-smirk smirk should buy another half-hour undisturbed. Staff found the expression infuriating, perhaps partly because photographers loved it. Sybille was a minor celebrity, part of a freak-glamour subculture that performed its picturesque disabilities for a different kind of camera eye, a jaded one savoring a divergent aesthetic. She'd always be exploited, but the public paid for the fetish show rather than sending bills. In here, as she was groomed for abuse, her family was charged for the privilege.

An international cripple-chic feature had showcased her on location in Finland and Arctic-coastal Norway, her enigmatic, fairytale looks captured in exotic Sámi-inspired outfits. All seven pages were framed on the walls of her room. It was pleasant to know staff had to see so many shadings of her face, smiling and out of reach, so close to her real home.

Breathing into her own harmonic, Sybille shifted, adapting to changes in her body since her hypermobile joints had begun to break down, following the trajectory written in her genetic code. Instead of slipping into a full lotus position, she now had to extend her worse leg in front of her and rest the other foot on top. She'd first learned meditation techniques to keep her blood pressure controlled. It had been low to the point of causing her to faint when she stood, but more recently, and for reasons she'd kept to herself, it had begun spiking. For the first time, she had something precious to protect, and she was the perfect vessel for secrets.

Doctors blamed one symptom or another on any of the genetic disorders accompanying her neurology; the diagnostics weren't as clear-cut as the profession implied. The same syndrome cluster, whatever it might contain of Ehlers-Danlos, Marfan, and the circulatory and immune comorbids thereof, was slowly crippling her and had created a potentially fatal heart condition, along with migraines, seizures, and uncertain fine motor control. It also made her body ethereally slender and her alabaster skin so translucent that every vein seemed visible.

Each breath said goodbye to the old meat-cage and greeted the new one. Another way to be a beautiful mutant could be marketed and weaponized. Her shining white-blonde hair remained faithful, and she could still wield her aquamarine eyes like katanas, efficient and remorseless.

Before the intrusion of the speaker, she'd gotten past thinking how near her eighteenth birthday was, and with it, emancipation. She'd be leaving the CareWell Behavioral Analysis and Remediation Institute forever, no more being controlled by her adoptive mother. In a couple of months, she'd be earning her own money, with her sister managing her career, but not yet.

Now, she needed to be in the moment, taking in everything the well could teach before she left. Her best friend at the institute, Rowena, a non-speaking nine-year-old with a disfiguring skin condition who'd died of exposure during an escape, could navigate better than most of the inhabitants. Their conversation could continue after she left the institute. The others were trapped deeper down, and these next few weeks would be her last chance to connect to them.

Each breath drew her toward the slope, until she felt the long slide begin. Mourning voices surged from vast darkness, first like lapping water on a breeze-brushed pond, then in more powerful, layered waves. The history of the place resonated with despair.

A yowl broke the cadence, forcing her backward and out as a huge black-furred shifter burst past, then through the blue-padded wall. It writhed as it ran, the stench confirming it was horribly burned. Sybille vocalized before she could stop herself, and then waited miserably for the lecture to come from the speaker. The equipment might pick up a faint static disturbance from the creature's agony, but nothing that would justify a sound from Sybille.

Rowena trailed after the injured shifter, turning to Sybille with her finger to her lips. Miming entering her words on a communication tablet, her mouth curved in a painful, complicated smile. *I did something for you. I'll have to show you later.*

Sybille put her hand over her mouth and spoke silently. *Did you get Dr. Fallowfield?*

Another horrible howl echoed through the walls, and Rowena vanished, her inhuman voice lingering in the absent space.

Later.

* * *

Not as jarringly exquisite as her companion, Artemida was striking—equally tall, a decade older, deliberately menacing in obsidian-dyed hair and steel-studded leather. The pair walked slowly along the bit of restored Victorian grounds of the Taconic Behavioral Health complex. Sybille used the oak-and-brass cane she'd have to surrender on re-entering the institute building. Winter wind scuffed their cheeks—still, Sybille hungered to be outside, even as the chill knifed into her joints.

Artemida looked up and murmured, "Everything still good with the pregnancy? Promise you'll see a doctor if you need one."

Sybille ran her hand down her torso and made a smiling "mmahmm" sound.

"Are you sure you're okay without your blood pressure meds? This isn't worth your life. Aortic dissection is nothing to fuck around with."

Covering her mouth, Sybille whimpered.

A pebble in the path clattered away, propelled by a sharp kick from Artemida's formidable boot. "You don't owe the spawn of an entitled swine the continuing abuse of your body. Pig!" She spat accurately at the pebble.

Nodding, Sybille took in the wide sky and low clouds rushing along the mountain ridge.

A commemorative plaque by their feet noted the overlapping foundations of two buildings—the classrooms of the St. Isaac Jogues Boarding School for Indian Youth, and an outbuilding of the Taconic State Hospital for the Mentally Infirm. The massive fieldstone remnants enclosed a small-scale reproduction of the old gardens. All the residential school structures had been demolished, and the remaining original asylum complex stood disused on the far side of the sweeping main road through the campus, off limits, the formal landscaping reduced to rusted chain-link fences, weeds, and gravel. Rowena's body had been found there, against the granite exterior of one of the deserted buildings.

Heavy coats offered cover for contraband. Artemida patted Sybille's ungloved hand, pressing a Russian-language communication tablet into it as she side-eyed the surveillance. They huddled in the windbreak of a foundation corner left shoulder-high. The women resembled photographic negatives of each other, mirrored leaning in, foreheads almost touching, long hair obscuring their faces. They were half-siblings, although no one but they and their birth mother knew it outside the pre-Magnitsky Act adoption system that had brought Sybille to the US.

Sybille retained her written birth language, but not its sound. Her adoptive family forbade Artemida to use Russian. Reading was never a problem; the child consumed English literature years beyond her supposed comprehension levels. She'd used typed communication precociously in the orphanage, but speech would never come, lost in the dyspraxic tangles of her neurology.

The CareWell Institute was the last hope for forcing her to seem normal. Fashion cachet was based in Sybille's freakishness, but full family status would eventually require not being embarrassing in public.

Communication devices were forbidden except during therapy sessions. Defying the Ranks' prohibition on assistive tech and the

Russian language, Artemida had secretly commissioned the tablet. Sybille's metallic-manicured fingers danced across the touchscreen programmed to compensate for her halts and tremors.

Cyrillic words showed in the text line of her sister's phone. *Why did you need to see me? Ranks likes it when she thinks we're fighting. You'll show in the visitor log.*

Tonie Ranks was Sybille's adoptive mother. The wealthy, childless American woman resented the sullenly competent teenaged "nanny" who'd been included in the package to help the Russian orphan adapt to her new surroundings. The arrangement was stipulated in the Murmansk Oblast Regional Administration foreign adoption contract.

Sybille's silence had been explained as a result of the shock of finding her fashion-model mother's suicide, but in the world behind the official one, her stripper mama with influential friends wasn't dead, just in detox. The neglected offspring needed to be placed, and the younger one was a rare prize if she wasn't examined closely. Under threat of opening a bidding war for the child, the agency laid down its terms for an expedited process. Sybille wouldn't be profitably adoptable once her idiosyncrasies could be diagnosed.

Artemida nodded and frowned. *Wish I didn't have to—she's turned me in for deportation, started proceedings to block emancipation. Institute supports her getting permanent guardianship. Mama found me a flat downtown near Kirovka. Will write, but probably won't reach you.*

9-week gestational DNA is with lawyer, paternity verified from Fallowfield's "genius sperm bank" genetic profile. Swine. Damages suit a longshot with Daddy disappearing. Institute pleads not responsible, claims you seduced him. Please abort if health problems. Not worth it.

The blood drained from Sybille's head, her ears rang, and the inside of her mouth turned to cotton. The sisters clasped hands tightly as she fought to blink away clusters of black floaters from her eyes.

* * *

Sybille rubbed her faux copper nails over the knot in her belly. The talons had grown out pink moons at the base, but they reminded her of the Arctic currents of home. Their scrape helped her ignore the water needles making her skin twinge and shudder. She hated showers. There was no lock on the communal washroom door, and she'd be observed minutely for days after Artemida's visit.

Her diagnosis—that she didn't know her own emotions—was horseshit. Words like "rage" and "rebellion" might take time to translate from mental images to written Russian, then English sounds typed out, but the fire in her guts and flesh was fierce and fully felt. Hamish Fallowfield had dismissed her fury with a psychoanalyst's authority the first time she tried to bite him. If she was supposed to lack awareness, then she'd hide behind her blank expression and seethe in privacy.

A staffer walked in without knocking. No annoyance escaped Sybille's alabaster mask as she wrapped her bird-skeleton of a torso in a miserly towel.

"Getting a little pot belly there, Ranks," the staffer snickered. "Maybe eat something besides potatoes and bread. I'll put that on your chart—time to revisit food aversions."

Turning her back, Sybille dropped the towel and pulled her robe on, but the staffer turned her by the shoulders and gestured for her to leave it open.

The staffer leaned forward to scrutinize Sybille's stomach.

Sybille swatted at the staffer's head and stepped back, vocalizing sharp, angry "nah" sounds.

The staffer's eyes flashed. "Pathological demand avoidance, you are our precious Sybbie. Mustn't trigger the princess's delicate sensory-processing issues with a proper slap in the face. No peas under the mattress for the director's favorite."

The institutional robe fell open, revealing the bloody gouges on Sybille's lower belly above the pale, damp gold of her pubic hair.

The staffer grabbed her wrists. "These nails come off *now*! Dr. Fallowfield isn't around to give you exclusions from your medicals, and this isn't going to fly with Dr. Rivers. She'll see you get properly examined for once."

* * *

Sybille's hands ached where they'd been gripped and spread. Anti-scratch sleeves, sewn-shut canvas tubes reaching her armpits, were securely fastened to a band around her chest. Even if she subluxated her shoulders, she couldn't wriggle free. One rotator cuff had been forced partway out while she was restrained face-down on the four-point board for her institutional manicure. It was the most roughly she'd been handled since she'd been at the institute.

Staff had reminded each other to be wary of leaving marks on her easily bruised skin. The shock harnesses most noncompliant kids wore were left off for the same reason. A week before she was booked to go to Milan, she'd been left with a ragged crimson burn-stripe halfway around her tiny, sharp-boned ankle, and her mother forbade the institute from using it again.

Wrapping her muffled arms around her ribs, she rocked herself in the dark, humming while she chewed her lip. There was a wide-angle infrared camera in her room, and she'd probably be yelled at for stimming, but she was too bludgeoned to care. No light showed under the door, although she couldn't muster enough curiosity to wonder why not.

The scent of singed flesh and fur entered the room. Something huge moaned.

The ceiling opened into vastness. Rowena always appeared outside of time, accompanied by celestial bodies, and for Sybille, she brought gifts. Their friendship had existed outside their physical years when both were in meat-cages, and like many autistic affections, had been labeled as inappropriate age-level bonding. Now free of those constraints, it had deepened.

Polaris hung overhead, surrounded by brighter but less constant circumpolar stars, directional indicators that never dipped below the horizon in the geometry of Sybille's heart.

"Arctic Circle" means "Circle of the Bears," the constellations *Ursa Major* and *Ursa Minor*, from the Greek αρκτικός (*arktikos*) "near the Bear," from ἄρκτος (*arktos*) bear.

Арктический

Home.

Luminous green and magenta curtains shimmered a hundred miles above, riding the lines of magnetic force. The boreal compass point accelerating erratically along the Canadian Arctic Archipelago, skittering toward Russia in anticipation of the great reversal when south will become north, turning directional instruments insane and electronic communications to gibberish. The aurora crackling, solar winds burning into Earth's atmosphere in the polar night.

Home.

Thank you. This is beautiful. What happened to the shifter?

Rowena—in the form she always appeared to Sybille, as the canny woman she would have become had she lived—reached out and replied in kind, silently. *He got forced into the machinery and became entangled.*

That must happen very often. The machinery is everywhere.

It always happens.

The shifters only came with death. If it was hers, Sybille was indifferent to it since she learned she'd never be free in her flesh. *Who have you come for?*

Uncertain. I've come to show you something, and then it will be decided.

Feeling herself stand up, Sybille looked down at the broken teenager rocking.

Rowena clasped her hand. *Hold on very tight.*

The shifter nuzzled his head under Sybille's other arm to support her.

Things could get strange.

They moved into pitch darkness, limping and stumbling. Sometimes staticky lines shot through the absolute black, and Rowena's body showed as the boy who'd hung himself. The stench from the shifter's burned, mangled foreleg made Sybille struggle to keep from retching.

A chuckle came from beside her. *Watch out for the dead cat. It bites. The physicists keep worrying at it.*

The ground became uneven, shuddering under Sybille's feet. This wasn't the smooth glide into the well, but she began to hear the same grieving waves. The sounds emanated from Rowena, who wore a faint necrotic luminescence under her mottled vitiligo.

Her guide smiled. *Shortcut. I am Legion.*

The landscape showed dim features. Another shifter, smaller and lighter-colored, crossed their path and circled around them. It gave several possessive-sounding warning yips, and the large one disengaged itself and followed its companion into the shadows.

Turning back to Rowena, the surge of nausea was too powerful for Sybille to push down. The glow now showed a fully rotting corpse. When she pulled her fingers from Rowena's grip, they were slick with putrefaction.

Sybille fought for reason. *Why? Why? Why?* The wailing came from everywhere.

Why did I kill myself? Why did I bring you here? Why do I look like week-old roadkill?

Unable to articulate, Sybille nodded.

Rowena made a hurrying gesture. *Okay, let's walk. I can't linger or*

I'll fall apart, and then you will *be in a rough spot. So, briefly, I have hell to pay for taking myself out of the flesh game. This is the borderland, and as long as I'm on the territory, I'm going native, like it or not.*

Sybille got up shakily. *I thought I was here before, but it wasn't like this.*

The ground swarmed with fat maggots, crushed, curling and oozing with every step, surging up their ankles. Rowena hummed pleasantly. It seemed to lull the anguished voices. The slippery churning under their feet turned to soft earth, and smelled more of clean humus. Huge trees towered over them, barely visible in a night forest.

The skin knitted back together on Rowena's face. *Better? Yes, you've been here, you just took another entrance.*

Taking Rowena's hand again, Sybille hurried alongside her. *You answered the last question, but not the others.*

They paused a moment, and Rowena pressed her forehead against Sybille's. *Do you see your future present? Got it? Now we have to run!*

Their feet moved so fast that they rose in the air. Below spread the landscape they'd been through, from the void where they'd entered the charnel lands to the lush forest floor. They cleared the treetops, swooping and soaring in a vast, deeply shadowed central courtyard of a building the size of an empire. Moonlight filtered from an open rectangle miles overhead. Windows rushed past like speeding trains or plummeting elevators with broken cables.

Rowena pointed out tiny figures in one, and their trajectory slowed. *Time is a distance that alters the shape of things.*

She adjusted their perspective so they looked down into the room as if through a skylight. *Behaviorists take anything you love and use it against you. The institute's goal is to extinguish the unwanted. I was less wanted than you.*

Below them, the nine-year-old Rowena, blotchy-skinned in aqua sweats and sparkly plastic sneakers, was strapped into a chair. A harness restrained her torso, and an anti-bite mask covered her mouth. A staffer screamed in her face. "NO! No more tablet! Use. Your. Words."

Sybille put her fingertips carefully to her friend's cheek in case ghosts could get touch neuralgia. *We must be indistinguishable from the peers they choose for us. I wouldn't mind being indistinguishable from you.*

Flapping her hands, Rowena turned her head away. *Too many feels. Sorry. I'll fast forward through a lot of "Touch your nose—good girl, have a gummy bear."*

A worn unicorn plush toy in the pale blue shade of Rowena's child-self's clothes floated benevolently over the scene. The restrained child struggled toward it.

A faceless staffer snatched it out of her sightline. Her voice was a thousand overlaid copies of nearly identical words with similar scripted, joyless inflections. *"No! You can't have the toy unless you stay STILL. Don't spin. Quiet hands. Moo like a cow for me, mmkay? It'll be fun, let's play a game!"*

Rowena gestured a hatchet-chop that opened up the composite staffer's thoughts in a seething mass. *"No? Of course not. Look me in the eyes, retard. Dear God, give me something I can put on the chart for this session. Nope, nobody to see here. Jeezus fuk—quit screeching, you brainless brat! When in hell will this day be over?"*

Institute therapists forced child-Rowena's clumsy fingers around small items, guiding her to place them in containers as they chirped in bleakly cheery voices. Hours dragged. Rowena kicked her glitter-spangled shoes, tried to take back her unicorn, wailed and hissed from behind the mask. There was hunger and thirst, and relief from them placed just out of reach. Days of hours and months of days passed, and she was dressed differently, and there were different ways she was kept in place.

Interdimensional Rowena fluctuated, appearing younger as her tears welled. *Forty hours a week, for eternity. They can't relent—that would be letting the retard win. If you try hard enough to comply, it starts again at the next level. If you resist, they do things to you. If you smile and play along, they don't make it as bad, but you hate yourself more. There is no horizon.*

Sybille held Rowena close. It felt like permafrost and electricity. *I understand.*

They spun vertiginously out of the moonlit courtyard and crashed into frozen dirt.

Good, because I gotta go now.

* * *

Sybille was on the far side of the drive, among the abandoned asylum buildings. A clear, gibbous moon hung midway up the sky. She had sparse memories of being a toddler enduring winter in a poorly heated apartment in the largest city above the Arctic Circle, but she couldn't remember ever being so cold. The wind scorched like dry ice.

Stumbling in thin snow, through bare, overgrown shrubs around the granite foundation of the most formal of the buildings, she searched for shelter. Something howled softly, grieving, and she followed the sound deeper into the thicket. The lame shifter stood guard next to what looked like a pile of clothes on the ground, but she knew what it must be. As she came closer, once-and-forever nine-year-old Rowena's blue-gray skin and tangled hair became clearer. Sybille curled next to her and clutched her stiffened hand, afraid if she gripped too hard, the fingers would snap off, brittle from the frigid night. The shifter vanished.

Feeling her way along the wall to the permeable place, Sybille passed through the stone into the building. The space became the vast courtyard again. Above, instead of the moon, was the pole star—more brilliant than on the other side, pulsing with a subtle heartbeat.

Sybille laid her hand on her belly with a faint smile. *Time to find Papa. Auntie Rowena put him in here somewhere.*

The ground dropped away as she rose, the regions spreading out below like a map. The place she needed to locate was almost as light-absorbing as the entry place, its terrain visible like the nighttime interior of a charred room after a fire. Polaris drew her like a compass needle, pulling from inside her toward a point certain.

She came to the place of partial permeations—where the comatose, hallucinators, dreamers, the senile and cursed were held until released into one side or the other. The terrain was formed from volcanic rock. She was looking for one vesicle among countless billions, but she moved with certainty. The ground was black and bubbled, with every blister containing a consciousness in flux.

The stars gave enough light to find the cell where Rowena had hidden the rapist who'd fathered Sybille's unborn child. Part of a much larger submerged orb protruded from the dull rock. Striking the exposed dome, she shattered it like an empty eggshell and leaned over the opening. The fragments clattered into the cavernous space. A gasp came from the void.

Sybille chuckled. Her voice emanated from her body in scaled reverberations, down into the chamber. *Would the Extinguished Gentleman like to come out?*

Dr. Hamish Fallowfield, onetime director of the CareWell

Institute, gasped again, tried to form words, and failed. Pulling back enough to allow the starlight into the space, Sybille could just make out his face. The rest of him seemed swallowed by the black rock.

She reached into the opening. *Come along, I have something to show you.*

A shriek tore the landscape, and Sybille dragged her prisoner through the rift that opened when she pulled him through. They were back in the Taconics, in late winter. Weak gray light trickled over a swampy meadow. At the edge were bare trees, and from one hung the frozen tatters of a body picked over by crows.

This is your new program, Hammy. Rowena designed it just for you, and she thought it was only right that I should explain it to you.

Your task is to complete this scenario so it can be found as you see it. No motion will be permitted that doesn't bring you closer to the completion of your assignment. It will take as long as required. You may approach the tree, fasten the rope, and finish the tableau. Attempting any other movement is futile. Time will freeze where it is, and you with it. You will become so familiar with the setting that you'll be able to perceive the sky stop turning when you fail. Once the initial act is done, you must maintain presence of mind within the disintegrating body in order for time to progress, up to the point you see here.

After that, who knows? We'd all love to move on.

* * *

Sybille watched herself. She needed to use the bare toilet in the corner, but the anti-scratch sleeves wouldn't allow her to undo the Velcro fastener on her pants. The monitor told her to stop attention-seeking when she wailed and tried to mime what she needed.

Laying her muffled fingers over her belly, she wondered if the sensation might be the baby quickening. A wave of protectiveness washed through her. Her unborn was her pole star; she swung around it without fathoming how it had come to be. Her strangely programmed flesh made its own decisions, and intervention had always brought more complications than relief.

She was dizzy, her head hurt, and her hands felt swollen inside the sleeves. She'd had borderline edema even though she'd been trying to eat better. Her missed periods never induced much interest because of her anorexia, but now she wondered if she might have preeclampsia. She decided she'd accept the medical examination, however traumatic.

The room spun, and her ears roared. For the first time, she regretted throwing away her blood pressure pills, but she wouldn't have been able to get to them anyway.

The center of her chest felt heavy and massive. The walls retreated into shadow, and brilliant light shone down. She crawled to the door and pounded on it.

With fading sight, she could make out a ring of shifters surrounding her. Heaviness became shearing pain like she'd never experienced. In those remaining seconds, she understood her mutant heart had torn itself open. Her body had completed its cycle. She keened for the unripened child dying inside it.

The monitor screamed at her to be quiet.

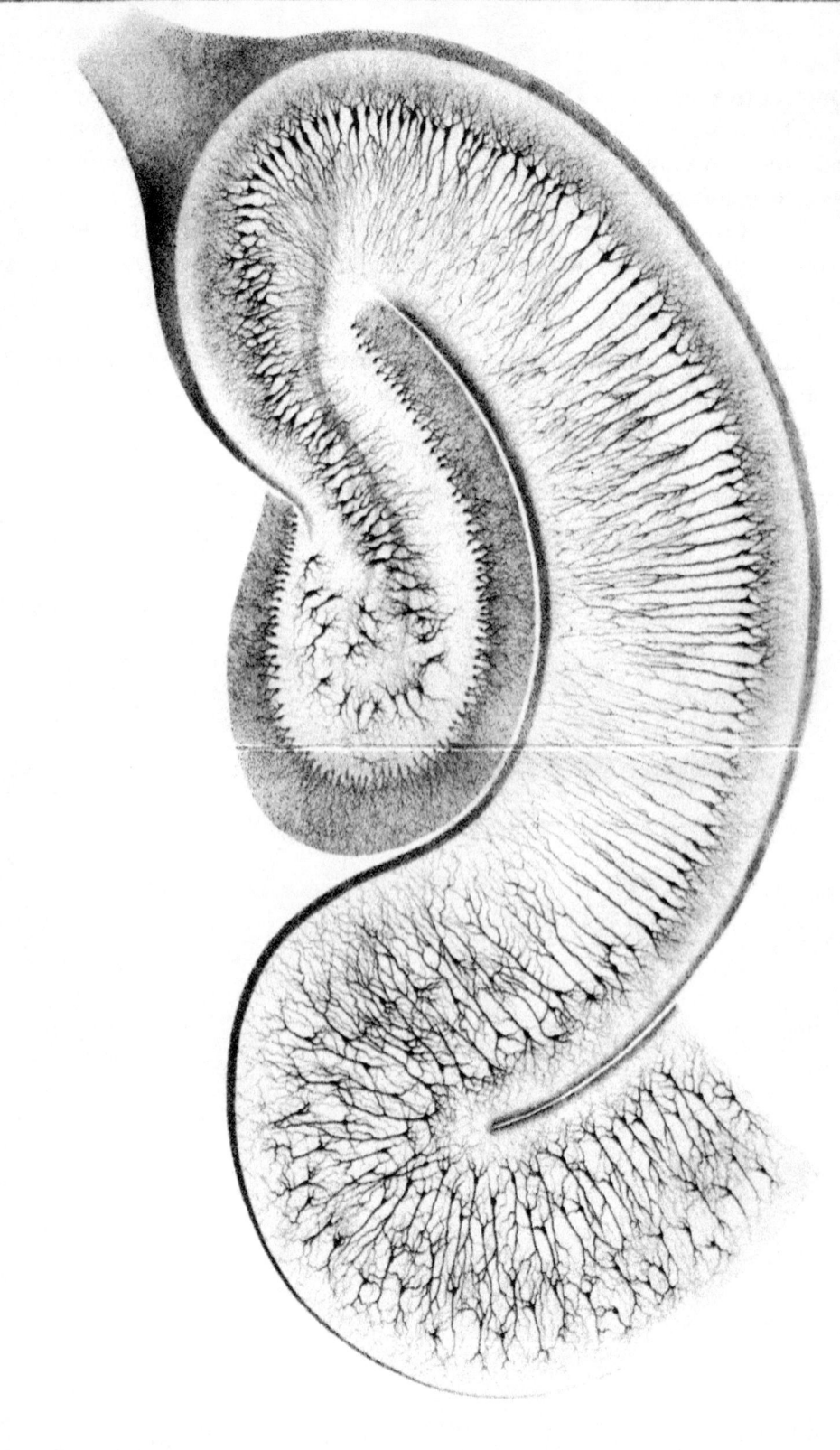

HAIR OF THE ONE THAT BIT
A Novella Structured on a Spenserian Sonnet

[I constructed this like a sonnet because the moth-eaten academic in me loves to play with form; every chapter is a line in the Spencerian scheme. It's about looking-glass wars. I think I might call it *And What Agnes Found There*, but I haven't decided yet. I don't really have the last few lines yet, but I expect they'll come to me.]

First Quatrain
1-Agnes

Agnes Pratt studied the quizzical face peering in the window at her. She couldn't quite place it, or remember exactly why she was looking out from this particular long, narrow view, somehow to have caught another's eye. The figure on the other side, lit by an overhead glare, extended a hand in response. Agnes jolted, realizing she'd been checking herself in the mirror in the alcove by her apartment door before leaving for work. She hadn't recognized the other someone wearing her tweed suit. Now she straightened it and nodded at her sturdy, tailored outline with grudging approval.

As she started to open the door, she felt her mouth twist into a bitter smile. She reached into the harsh shadow cast by the shelf above the coat rack for her charcoal-colored anorak.

4:30 AM, Upstate New York, February...think you might need a coat, Aggie? Too early for sane folk to be out and about. Time has never been kind. It's just the passage of it, like a freight train forever running over one's weary face. Tends to get harder to register the damage until it catches you by surprise.

Still, the unwelcome echo of mirrors in her mother's house. Nine years old, watching the pair of visiting nurses covering them in crisply creased bedsheets. Plain white linens pulled from the closet, scented faintly with the lingering tang of bleach underneath the lavender-water. No matter how busy she might be with other things, Mama would mist the warm fabric with cologne herself as it lay on the ironing board. She'd then fold each spreading, fragrant pile into a tidy rectangle before it cooled and wrinkled. The maids could never be trusted to do it properly. Agnes balanced herself, breathing in the good memory of clean, dark shelves behind louvered doors.

[Order. Stability. Virtù (in the Machiavellian sense—that is, to act bravely, decisively, and with ruthless pragmatism for the benefit of what is held dear, not necessarily to do what is "good" in itself).]

Sometimes she regretted selling the handsome Plattsburg early Victorian, but it was a heavy upkeep burden for a single woman, as well as a hellacious commute down a lot of miles of Interstate 87 to the CareWell Institute, particularly on a snowy day like this. Besides, there was no one who loved the old place enough to leave it to. The smug, distant cousins in California with their impeccable mid-century modern tastes would prefer the nice sum she'd gotten for it over a lifetime commitment to repointing bricks and repairing hand-carved woodwork. Let alone the snow clearing. Let them have their wildfires and mudslides. They might not know it yet, but she'd made sure they wouldn't see a dime.

The doctor had ordered the draping so Mama wouldn't startle at her own reflection and think a stranger was confronting her. Hardening of the arteries, they called it then, tragic in a woman not yet fifty, still physically vibrant, with a young child. A child who arrived later in Mama's life than was considered wise for a firstborn. Mama had often murmured that it had been a mistake to keep the pregnancy when there were so many reasons to let the barren old tree wither quietly; the fruit could yet break the brittled branches...

Mama. Always becoming someone else. Receding...

I wasn't worth her making any kind of effort to stay, I suppose. She just jumped down that rabbit hole like she heard someone a lot more interesting than me calling her.

Touching the reflection, Agnes reminded herself to practice self-compassion. It wasn't her fault her mother forgot her, nor was it her mother's.

Dementia is cruel. Mama hadn't had a choice in the matter, even if it might have seemed so. Not the only one who'd had their wits depart from under that roof either. Mama's uncle digging trenches and stringing barbed wire in the ravaged garden, muttering about the Great War. Except he hadn't been the one who fought in it; it was his own father who'd returned shellshocked, fumbling around for how to be a parent to his son. The boy had spent his childhood handing pliers to and hauling dirt-filled buckets away for his daddy as he dug in search of some kind of safety, and the habit had stuck in his memory, crowding out the world around him. Then he took over excavating the earthworks, the collapsed remnants of which had to be filled in with a backhoe before the house could be sold. Early-onset Alzheimer's. Tends to run in families.

Leaning in closer to the silvered glass, Agnes studied her alien face.

Acting director. Hmph. CareWell Institute, Acting Director. Interim appointment until someone better can be located...

Dear Lord! What's the time?! How long have I been standing here like an idiot?

* * *

[It took a while to "find" this character. Hard to locate a sympathetic core of a person who could treat your friends like she did. Autistics are supposed to lack empathy, and so we shouldn't write characters for shit. And I'm not just wrapped with a fey indigo wisp of autism either; I don't use mouth-speech.

Nonetheless, it's my job now. You can tell me if I did it right. I'll be around.]

* * *

Agnes squinted into the morning darkness, her SUV's defroster running full blast and the wipers swatting away sprays of sparkling flakes. She patted the visor clip St. Christopher medal quickly without taking her eyes off the road.

It was a short drive to the institute; in kinder weather she'd often walked there. It was as much hassle to scrape the ice off and let the thing warm up as it would have been to slog through the calf-high drifts and let the storm sting her face, but she didn't want to be seen entering the building like that. She was expected to be there before the daytime staff arrived, even though she was nominally in charge of the entire facility and could have delegated the responsibility.

Leave the messes unresolved, then dump them on me. Make sure it'll cost me more not to do it myself. Brats. The lot of them. Whichever side of the locks and cameras they're on.

The glassed-in pedestrian bridge that served as a gate to the Taconic Behavioral Health complex glowed ahead, its campus spreading graciously up rounded hills on each side, snow cover undisturbed by jaywalkers cutting through so early in the day. Mountains loomed as shadows in the rearview mirror, no hint of morning sun at their summits yet.

To the right, the old part of the complex sat mostly unlit, the drafty cut-stone Victorian buildings used for storage while the combined boards of directors of the current tenants fought with the local historical review committee over the right to tear the useless hulks down. It would be one thing if they'd been maintained; the once-handsome executive offices had been designed by a distinguished architect. Now they stood as a humiliating reminder of the psychiatric practices they'd championed.

[Yep. Good old Agnes, like she didn't use modern versions of the same treatments for uppity, inconvenient, lesser ones of us in her own work.]

Not to mention the attractive hazard the not-quite ruins represented. The graffiti and all that untrimmed shrubbery still left around the administration building. Perfect place for a child to hide. *That granite-headed little biter brat.* Agnes felt the recent scar along her nose. *Should have worn my Kevlar gloves. Might not have helped. Never expected she'd go for my face.*

Vitiligo, strange-looking little half-albino beast.

No one yet taking responsibility for letting her elope. And right after that Miles kiddo got himself...

Black eye for the institute's reputation she slipped out and froze to death against the foundation of that decrepit edifice. No tracks in the snow even to show how the hell—*Hush, Aggie. No need for words like that, even to think them*—how she got over to that side of the grounds.

What was that child's name again...?

[Rowena. That would be me. Ro for short. Not a child anymore, exactly, although I play one in your mind, bitch.]

* * *

Agnes wiped steam from her glasses on her way to her office. The loud, angry wailing of a recalcitrant non-verbal child reverberated from a classroom down the hall.

Every staff member knew that kind of extended outburst was unacceptable. Also, it was far too early for the classrooms to be in use. Agnes kicked off her snow boots and stomped out in her stocking feet, not taking the time to put on her office shoes.

She padded along the fluorescent-lit corridor, trying to locate the sound. One of the fixtures buzzed. Brian Nichols was supposed to get that fixed. He'd lectured her on how fluorescents were painful to autistics because they could perceive the buzz and flicker even when the things were working properly. Well, not lectured, but there was inappropriate lack of deference. Familiarity. He never would have spoken to Dr. Fallowfield so informally, as if Agnes didn't keep up with the research. Fluorescent lighting was the standard for commercial and educational facilities, and the children would have to adapt to it sooner or later. They might as well learn how to in the place that was supposed to prepare them for engaging in as much real life as they were capable of handling.

[Fuck you.

If I'd lived, I would have become a respected academic. How about that? One of the things the Devil shows you to punish you for daring to take your own life on your own terms turns out to be what you could have made of yourself if you'd had the backbone to keep on living. Welcome to Hell.]

Agnes snagged her tights on the corner of a lifting linoleum tile. She'd crossed over that same spot a hundred times in the last few weeks in her sturdy shoes and hadn't noticed it. Soon a pale pink baby toenail emerged through the laddered navy knit.

A distant door-slam announced the arrival of the first of the morning crew. She couldn't be seen like that.

Whatever the voice was, it wasn't from any of the classrooms. They were all empty. She'd turned the lights on in each one to satisfy herself of that. Thoughtfully making sure none of the early staff would be faced with entering a dark room gave her an excuse to be out in the hallway should someone come upon her and think she was wandering about for no reason.

The complaining yowl began again, from a different direction than she'd first thought. Either that, or the source was moving. If one of the clients was loose in the building, the consequences...

Miles... Rowena...

[Getting waaaarrrmer...]

Another, even more agitated sub-human howl of inarticulate fury.

Oh, hell and biscuits! Did another little wretch get left in the time-out rooms?

Agnes bolted down the main corridor and turned the corner to the row of closet-sized padded cubicles where unruly clients were left to safely calm down when necessary. Well, mostly safely. Miles was such a monkey, climbing like no child should...

Blinking against the darkness, Agnes pushed something half-seen out of her eyes and reached for the light switch. The fluorescents surged on with a high-frequency humming buzz. The sobs of raging displeasure distinctly came from the cubicle Agnes least wanted to open.

Oh for heaven's sake! Who left—

[Peek-a-boo.]

2-Brian

The dog kept approaching through the tall, dry grass, black against waves of bleached gold, late evening clouds scudding behind him, but he never got closer. Brian's whistle was lost on the hard breeze, and the dog's broad, bony head would turn as if he heard something else from another direction. Sometimes his long forelegs appeared, churning at full speed through the whipping stems. The rustling of the dream-field roared in Brian's ears, and the pre-storm wind stung his face.

He'd been here often enough to know not to look down.

* * *

[That's the thing about Brian, he's always on the verge of getting it—gets so much, but always seems to leave off right at the moment he could break through the thin place. Some part of him knows he's going to keep having this fucking dream until he does.

I love him dearly, and he's a good man who's earned it. A combat medic, among other things, never hesitated to go in where he was needed. Something inside him is dying though, and I'm trying my damndest to keep that from happening. I don't want him making eye contact with the Abyss on my watch.

He knows he's surrounded by energies he barely feels even when they kick him hard. Personal experience with that one. Will try to be as reliable a witness as I can on this. Make it interesting while I keep it true. The terms of my sentence if I ever get out of here.]

* * *

The faint glow of the day-and-date clock brightened faithfully at 5:00 AM. Brian had left it on its work schedule even though he hadn't been in for a couple of weeks. He had the feeling someone had been in the room, like he'd been in the orderlies' lounge at CareWell and fallen asleep. A glance at the clock dispelled the feeling.

I'm a free man, better or worse.

Moe purred and nuzzled against his chin, the morning stubble apparently serving as a grooming substitute for a cat's rough tongue.

Spitting long white hair, Brian gently pushed Moe down to his lap and sat up. "Okay, buddy. Breakfast is coming."

The animal was deaf, but he reacted with louder purrs.

Driving that girl to the institute every day had kept Brian within some kind of guardrails, but sometimes rails need to be jumped. After he'd told Krysta she had to find another way to get to work, he'd begun looking over his situation.

There was enough heating oil in the tank to last a couple months, and his woodpile was about half-left. The electric bill was always low, most of a butchered deer was still in neatly wrapped packages in the freezer, he'd gotten new tires that fall, and as long as Moe didn't need the vet, his bank account would hold out at least until late spring.

The McCoy couple up the road could be relied on in an emergency. Cindy McCoy had offered to help him navigate getting on disability and whatever paperwork he'd need for the veterans support agencies that had helped him in the past. He didn't like to draw on that well when he didn't have to, but it was comforting to know it was there.

Morningstar McCoy was a bit older than Brian and had a bad left arm, but could do most physical things better than the average person a decade younger, and he had Cindy, which was something to have, even if Cindy went her own way sometimes. Morn had mentioned more than once, almost like he was proud of it, that she had preferences he couldn't fulfill, as if it was perfectly ordinary that one's wife might be away for a while, indulging in temporary same-sex companionship. It was an understanding between spouses that Brian didn't inquire on.

Morn and Cindy were the only other permanent human residents on Abenaki Ridge. Brian's woodlot acreage and the McCoy farmstead had been passed through generations of their respective families, and though there was no blood kinship, the familiarity was in their bones. Brian couldn't have said whether he liked his neighbors or not; they were neighbors, and close neighbors in the rural Taconics are more valuable than close friends who live on the far side of the mountains.

He and Morn had talked about setting up a radio connection since Brian had given up the outage-plagued landline.

Maybe it's time for that. Have the license, might as well use it.

He only used his mobile phone for work anyway, and he'd kept it shut off for the last ten days so the mailbox would fill up and spill over in silence.

First it had been his immediate supervisor with petty threats, then middle management's peeved entreaties, up to Assistant Director Dr. Pratt and her oleaginous appeal. "You love the children and they know it. They're constantly asking about where that nice Mr. Nichols has gone."

Somehow he'd become a valued member of the team.

If you vultures actually want to keep your employees, try treating them like they're worthy of a little respect.

Brian scowled and stared out the trailer window at the faint shimmer of pre-dawn snow.

First one deep enough to bring out the big state plows, not that they'd ever come up Abenaki Ridge.

* * *

[A little backstory—the institute was built on the old-school behaviorist doctrine that its neurodivergent juvenile "students" were nothing more than sealed units, black boxes whose interiors were invisible and irrelevant, differing only in the specifics of their steering mechanisms.

Under classic behaviorism (and, although it's played down by its practitioners, its widely practiced offshoot, applied behavioral analysis, or ABA), the control levers of the black box are those things to which it is averse and which can be imposed on it, and those things which it desires, which can be withheld from it.

Act bad, get nasty thing; act good, get nice thing. Simple. The objective is the black box-subject's compliance, and to make it understand that the trainer will never, ever relent.

When the behavioral therapist moves these levers to manipulate the black box, the technique is called operant conditioning. Eventually, the use of these levers would be expected to condition the student into appropriate models of conduct. This is known as compliance training.

Consistent, unrelenting application of behavior-modification techniques can be remarkably effective, so long as the subject's trauma, loss of dignity, and damaged personal boundaries aren't considered.

Yes, your narrator has skin in this game, metaphorically at this point, since the skin of my body is long gone and the coverings I wear now are far more versatile. It is not pleasant to be subjected to such meticulous dehumanization. That's why I bit Agnes Pratt when I was nine years old, after one too many forty-hour weeks as a black box moving pennies around on a fucking table under my compliance program. It's why I felt hope when I knew I was dying.]

* * *

The ancient snowblower coughed, seized, and came to life, emitting a sound like a commercial coffee grinder with a pebble in it. On his way to the institute a few summers back, Brian had pulled the two-stage Ariens from a roadside trash heap just beyond the stretch of manicured farms near town and heaved it into the bed of his truck. Always alert to glints of bright paint on rusted metal, he usually kept his workshop behind the trailer full of the carefully dissected results of his scavenging. In the last year, his inventory had fallen off as his salvage stops were curtailed.

It was an honest craft, equipment restoration, and he looked forward to getting back to it. In more productive times, it had been a nice supplemental income.

Spend half a day and about fifteen bucks in parts, get a machine that'll serve for maybe another decade if it's taken care of.

That was before Krysta, who would emit panicked whining

noises at the thought of being late for work if he so much as slowed down to look at a promising bit of scrap. Precious little Krysta, Agnes Pratt's fresh-faced assistant.

It seemed as though the whole ridge had gone still while she was there. There were things that used to pass along the spine of the low mountain, things felt more than perceived, some friendly, some not, some pretending to be other than what they were. Feral canines that filtered through the woods around his house without leaving tracks, children's voices chattering in an incomprehensible language carried on the wind. It wasn't like Krysta intended it to happen, but just by being around, she'd caused those doors to be shut by what preferred to stay behind them for its own reasons. Something in him had gone empty with their absence.

Now there were other things. The spirits of the ridge had never felt personal before, but whatever few that remained knew his secrets. And then there was that last time. Abenaki Ridge Road had more than made up for its stillness with that one.

Well, enough ruminating. Plenty of time to stew after dinner on the warm couch with the cat. Work to do right now.

He hadn't seen Krysta's car go by in the time he'd been AWOL. Maybe she was staying in town. Better place for her. As he cleared the lower part of the drive, he snagged an auger blade on a hidden ridge of frozen gravel and snapped a shear pin. Easing into a painful kneel, he pulled off a glove with his teeth and fumbled in his coverall pocket for a replacement and his Leatherman.

Cracked and callused, his fingers felt like numb extensions of the frozen metal he struggled with. The multitool slipped into the snow under the machine as he tried to insert the new pin. His old Desert Storm back injury and a whole new chorus of aches and dings from his recent tumble while hunting objected to the quick grab he made for it. There was no way around having to get down on all fours to look for the damned thing.

Shifting on his knees, he caught sight of a familiar figure walking in the road, coming down from where it ended at the crest of the ridge.

Cindy McCoy waved and called a greeting whose details were lost in the falling snow.

Waving back, Brian didn't bother to yell anything into the white air.

Cindy broke into a trot, flumes of fresh powder flying up around her work boots. She was a tall woman, handsome, maybe Brian's age, maybe a bit older, maybe even older than Morn, but not stooped the way Brian had started to get. She'd appeared at Morn's farm one day nearly thirty years ago, and there was never a question of her leaving again.

With a couple loping strides, she was kneeling beside Brian. Gloveless, she plunged her long, weathered hands into the snow a few times like a predator hunting rodents.

She pushed a strand of graying auburn hair out of her face and held the Leatherman up triumphantly. "Got it!" She tossed it to him, raising an eyebrow when he almost dropped it again. "Here, you hold the pin in place. Let me do the finagling. You'll never get it, stiff as you are. You might like to think you're recovered from that number you did on yourself, but ask for an assist sometimes maybe, Bri. I know we've got no tenants right now, but we can get someone over if you'd give us the chance." She smiled as if to ease the punch of her words. "Morn's always collecting some kid or other who thinks he's interested in farming old-school—for a few weeks anyway."

After they got the part replaced, Brian accepted her grip on his wrist as he heaved himself to his feet. "Thanks. I'll keep it in mind. The Pettiman girl isn't renting from you anymore?"

"Krysta was never gonna be a good fit." Something with an edge to it crossed Cindy's face. "So I guess you didn't know?"

Brian had sometimes wondered if Krysta might be one of Cindy's off-the-record amusements. Cindy never seemed to let her emotions seep into her flower-picking, but Krysta was too much of a baby to grasp the distinction, and the way she'd gone on about Cindy had made him hope the older woman wasn't taking advantage of the younger one's infatuation.

Keeping his eyes low while he brushed off his legs, he invited her inside. "Come on and get those fingers warmed up around a cuppa. You can tell me about it in the kitchen. How you don't have chilblains never wearing gloves I'd like to know."

***

[Ah, yes. Brian's fall. More to come on that. But later.]

3-Agnes Again

[Like Brian, Agnes teeters, not on the edge of grasping something, but on the edge of embracing it with eyes open. Brian has started falling in one direction. We'll see about Agnes. Once she gets up off the floor, that is, and thinks about how she wet herself while running around in snagged tights and no shoes.

I do like to leave a memorable impression.]

* * *

The time-out room had been empty. Agnes assured herself of that again and again. With fingers trembling on the touchpad, she reviewed footage from the newly replaced camera system on her laptop. Her heart rate was still far too high, and every time she closed her eyes, what she saw made it race again.

She checked her messages. Nothing from Brian Nichols. Still.

The CareWell Institute was even more short-handed than it had been before Covid, and she'd thinned the herd herself, much as she hated to lose another staff member.

Krysta had been much too nosy. The girl had an overwhelming urge to dig up juicy stories just for the love of dirt. The Fallowfield drama had been too much temptation. Agnes hadn't been positive about the nature of the snooping until the end, but the snare she'd set revealed it.

["Fallowfield?" you ask. More about him later too.]

On the other hand, Brian had been reliable and incurious about the workings of his employer, though she hadn't yet debriefed him on what he knew about Krysta's death.

She listened to the last message she'd been able to leave on Brian's phone. "Brian, dear. Agnes Pratt here. Even if you've decided to move on from CareWell, at least let us know that you're all right. If you have some pressing personal need, we want to work with you—" The recording had cut off there; the inbox was full, and the recipient's phone was no longer connected to backup storage in the CareWell system.

Someone had removed the app, even though keeping it installed and updated had been a requirement of employment. Brian wouldn't have the technical skills to have done it on his own.

She'd been careful with her phrasing. She mustn't antagonize him in a way that would cause him to vent to someone with more of an agenda. The message could only be read as an expression of care and compassion for a troubled employee. Replaying it once more, she confirmed that to herself.

* * *

Kelli Rivers gave Agnes the kind of side-eye that only a marathon-running, Hermès scarf-wearing forty-ish professional with a clear shot at the top of her field could give an older colleague with a plus-sized, off-the-rack wardrobe and no visible path for advancement.

Agnes returned her own version of the look, with a strange tinge to it.

Careful, you vain little twat. I have no desire to take the directorship away from you, but keep it up and I'll re-think that.

"Dr. Rivers?" The young staffer who'd been working twelve-hour shifts to cover part of Brian's workload nervously waved a clipboard. "I can see you and Dr. Pratt are busy, but the state inspectors want more information, and I can't stall them again. They said they'll get a subpoena. This just came in by fax, so I don't have the electronic file yet—"

"I'll handle it—" Speaking over each other, the two CareWell Institute assistant directors reached for the papers. Kelli Rivers got there first, but Agnes neatly snatched them out of her hand, giving Kelli a raised eyebrow that said if she wanted them back, she was going to have to resort to physical violence in front of witnesses.

I believe I shall enjoy this game we've started. Now that Fallowfield is gone, your skinny flanks are dangerously exposed.

* * *

Agnes's low-heeled shoes clicked softly in the empty hallway. The heavy, locked doorknob to Hamish Fallowfield's office had a film of dust. The investigators had taken away anything useful weeks ago. The place that had been the hub of so much brilliance was an abandoned storefront in a decaying town.

Too devoted? Perhaps. Emotions aren't as steady as they once were.

Is my mind what it was, and was it ever what I thought? Getting too clever for myself.

Was Hames worthy of it? Yes. Warts and all.

Dr. Hamish Fallowfield, founder and sitting director of the institute. Up to the point he disappeared, the guiding light of CareWell. Known to produce results, dramatic changes in previously intractable juveniles. Controversial, but the institute never lacked clients. Salesman to wealthy parents, corporate donors, insurers, and government-funding agencies, at the apex of his profession. Vain and provocative enough to display a framed certificate acknowledging his "deposit" to an elite sperm bank dispensing the seed of only the highest-achieving males to the most carefully screened and selected breeding stock. After checking behind it, the police had left that hanging, albeit crookedly, on his office wall.

Why had he suddenly and thoroughly vanished?

The Sphinx is silent.

Questions swirled, from the coffee shops and galleries of the town nearby to the cramped offices of disability rights lawyers in several states who'd been trying to get Fallowfield's projects shut down for decades. They'd never gotten to him though. Not yet, anyway.

Hames, you really did fuck up. Ugly word, but appropriate.

And, ah, his pampered protégé, the stylish Dr. Kelli Rivers.

Rivers might have her papers published in the appropriate journals, but Agnes, whose degree came with an emphasis on clinical practice, kept the institute operational. One needed to understand which were the weak links before putting one's trust in the chain.

That meant knowing which staffers were having marital troubles and who was drinking secretly during lunch. She tracked employee expenditures and ride service use with the help of a custom app that burrowed deeply and silently in their personal lives. The app was also on the devices of senior administration, worming its way into their tablets and phones when they accessed files from the institute's servers.

A pair of young staff therapists giggled as they walked by, regurgitating some show they were going to binge re-watch.

Do you silly children believe in anything you do, or is it just the paycheck keeping you coming back?

Too tarnished now to attract anyone of real caliber to work here. And that's a tragedy. No one will want it on a resumé as long as I'm at the helm.

Let the squabble go, Aggie. If it's going to survive, this place needs a bright light at the top, and it ain't you. You can keep the twat on a short leash, but let her have the spotlight.

The leash would be there, invisible. Every person's weak spots, private connections, habitual and unusual movements known to her, a woman so dull as not to be worth looking at.

No back doors left open to her own vulnerabilities. Once she had a comfortable grasp of the app and its layers of functionality, the non-verbal autistic teen CareWell client who'd designed it in exchange for unlimited internet access and the privilege of leaving his room light on after 9:00 PM had a fatal seizure.

Agnes was knowledgeable in the dosage and effects of psychoactive and central nervous system medications. So many of the institute's clients had unfortunate comorbidities that required a well-stocked pharmacy.

* * *

As Agnes passed through the lobby, her phone dinged with a priority notification. Kelli Rivers, with something about attending an online meeting with a client's family in her place.

Let the little viper handle her own administrative load for a change.

She left the text unanswered. An anxious-looking couple in matching tartan face masks and expensive coats waited by the information desk with their hands in their pockets, not standing too close to the polished walnut.

The receptionist called over, "Dr. Pratt, the Staffords had an appointment for 9:30, but the roads were so bad they just got here. Dr. Rivers was supposed to take them through, but she's in a client conference. Could you show them around?"

"Always pleased to play native guide." Agnes started to extend her hand, but noticed the couple's slight recoil. After pulling up her own surgical mask, she patted it reassuringly. "We're all up to date with our shots here. We don't tolerate any of that nonsense."

* * *

The couple, their masks around their chins, looked at each other, the woman's eyes swimming with hope. The man looked exhausted after the ninety-minute tour, the weariness expressing itself as sour lines along the sides of his mouth.

Agnes nodded, her gesture taking in the full gibbering, flashing glory of the reward arcade. "We work magic here!"

With a quick wink, she pressed a red button camouflaged by an oversized playing card painted on the power box. Depressing the center of the five of diamonds made the towering, waistcoated animatronic white rabbit in the alcove beside her lurch forward, repeatedly bringing a pocket watch up to its face as it emitted an electronic wail of distress. "I'm late! I'm late! I'm late..."

The thing rode its ten-yard track to the end, lowered its arm, and glided unsteadily back into the alcove, its path protected by a bunting-festooned railing. Agnes extended open palms toward the couple. "So, do you feel our CareWell might be a good fit for your Ethan?"

"It seems too good to be true. We wanted to see this place as soon as we could. We haven't had time for background research, but I'm sure from the quick look at your website that it will be fine." The woman looked up at her husband. "We can't keep Ethan home much longer. It was hard enough to find someone willing to look after him for a few hours so we could visit you."

A shadow crossed the man's face. "All this...the lights...noises and such. The kids don't mind it?"

The woman frowned at him. "It's such lovely fun, Howard. Ethan needs to brighten up, and so do you."

Agnes watched the miniature drama open up.

Yes, the lovely fun is for you, Mommy. Not for your monstrous son and his obviously autistic father, fixated on their own centers while they suck the sunlit life out of you. Daddy just hides it better. Too bad we weren't able to catch him before he passed his toxicity on to the next generation.

The man shuffled. "So...the kids...when they get a good report, they get tokens. Right? And then they can buy...stuff. From these..." He waved at the kiosks and the entrances to the three arcades, each one aimed at a different stage of childhood to adolescence.

After making sure he wasn't going to add to his haltingly articulated question, Agnes nodded. "Yes. They can purchase plays for games from the arcade they've been assigned, or maturity-level appropriate toys. If the parents have given permission, they can also choose from a menu of little tasty treats that—"

Scowling, the man turned away from his wife's eyes. "I know you love all this, Emily, and it would make you happy, so you think it will make Ethan—"

"Oh! Damnit, Howard! Just damn it all! You take him then! You change his fucking diapers! Do you know how much shit there is in a thirteen-year-old's diapers, when he's close to two hundred pounds? Do you? Do you know how close I am to just leaving the two of you to your little cardboard houses and finding my life again?" The woman's explosion seemed to have drained her. She leaned against the wall with her head pressed between her hands, breathing in hard, dry gasps as if even her tears had withered away.

Agnes assessed the father's face and reconsidered the hug she'd been about to offer his wife. Something in him had changed to a harder, weightier persona.

"Those scale models are of the buildings I design, Emily. As you know, I prefer them to computer renderings for a final presentation. So do my clients, who pay for your lifestyle. I've come to realize our son does not fit with that lifestyle as you envision it. Ethan is far more interested in my work than you are, I think. On balance, it might be better if I found someone to come in and help with his needs and relieved you of that. It would be far less expensive than this sensory nightmare... And, yes, I take your point. I should do more toward his hygiene in any case."

Agnes watched and waited.

Emily took her husband's hand. "Howard, if you mean that, I'll work with you. You understand Ethan better than I do, and if you think he'd hate it, sending him here is not okay. I do care about your career, and our son; every aspect of him is a part of the life I want. I just need some help. I'm so exhausted, I could fade out into a pile of ashes."

Oh, good lord. You took the bait. How long will he keep up the act this time? Just enough to reel you back in. Next, she'll breed herself to him again and make another one.

Howard wrapped his arms around his wife and smoothed her hair as she sobbed against his chest. "Of course, Em, of course, of course we'll find the services. We'll find them. I'll be more helpful. No prevarications..."

Agnes waved an orderly over to see the Staffords out once they were done sniffling their way through renewing their marriage vows in the middle of her arcade hallway.

***

Kelli's anger seemed unpleasantly genuine. She stood in front of Agnes's desk and leaned in toward her, muscular hands splayed out just inches from Agnes's ample body. "So you lost the Stafford placement. I was on that account as soon as I learned their kid lost his slot at Upstate Behavioral—"

"Well, your client conference was just too important for you to stand around waiting for a late appointment, even one fully justified by the weather conditions." Agnes folded her arms, claiming her space, ready to engage.

"And do you know why I wasn't able to meet them, Agnes? I did ask you to take the helm on that teleconference, and you didn't bother to return my text. Another family with 'questions' about what the state inspectors might be looking into. Word gets around, you know. We do our best to plug all the leaks, but this ship is taking on a dangerous amount of seawater." Kelli pulled back, cooling her tone. "You swiped those papers before I had a chance to look at them, so I was just a tad unprepared."

A disagreeable knot began to form in Agnes's stomach. She held her tongue.

"Agnes, you of all people should know how many client placements we've lost in the last fiscal. Four dead kids and a counselor in less than two years does not look attractive, period. Now the Russian girl's birth sister has collared Antoinette Ranks into joining in a wrongful death suit even though those two despise each other. The loss of Sybille's modeling income wasn't pocket change. Tonie Ranks has the damages figured out to the dime, I'm sure. Apparently there was a *Vogue* France shoot coming up for another one of those dreamy retard-in-fairyland pieces, and now the magazine wants its advance back. The lawyers haven't seen our books yet, but they're trying. Maybe we need to settle before they do that."

Okay, that's not good. Hames needs to get back here and deal with his mess.

Agnes frowned, waiting for Kelli to stay in one place.

Tonie was reliable. Strong mother, adopted the orphan, found she'd been misled about the girl's condition and sent her here as soon as she saw it was necessary. Thought she had that Artemisia or whatever her name was deported. How did Tonie get hooked into taking in the older sister anyway? Au pair indeed, horrid witchy girl. Would've loved to give that one a few weeks in here.

Kelli was still going, pacing around Agnes's office with tight, caged-panther steps. "And do you know what else Artemida's lawyers want me to cough up, Agnes? They want the pharmaceutical log. Filed a complaint with the state for good measure. For some reason, I can't access the master folder to turn it over. Why *is* that, Agnes? You told the coroner the Pettiman girl must have gotten into your medication locker." She gestured toward the thick glass of the secure cabinet. "They took your word for it, but now the higher-ups want to see the whole picture, and I can't seem to show it to them."

"Well, tell them Hamish had the passwords and he didn't share them. He's not around to contradict you." Agnes felt lightheaded, but she had her bearings.

"Why should I do that, Agnes? What would make me want to lie for you? I know he always went to you for access to the records, not the other way around. I'm thinking maybe I need to make a separate peace while I can, not cover for you and your messes."

"Hmm. Why should you do that, Kelli? I wonder..." Agnes slipped her phone from the inner pocket of her white coat and refreshed it. She set it on the desk and spun it to face Kelli.

Kelli leaned in. The photo had been taken at a bar or club that obviously catered to lesbians. It showed Kelli on a makeshift throne, being fawned over by a half-dozen young women; there was a liberal use of tongues in the adoration.

Laughing, Kelli snatched the device up. "Oh, thanks. Going to forward this to myself if you don't mind. I love this pic, thought I'd lost it. The good old days."

Before Agnes could make her way around the desk, Kelli had accessed the photo messaging and entered an email address. She evaded Agnes's lumbering pursuit while scrolling through the gallery. Finally, Agnes got her cornered.

Holding the phone over her head, Kelli crowed, "I'm at least three inches taller than you, Agnes, you old sow. You'll never reach it. Your blackmail portfolio is twenty years out of date. At least read a few social attitudes polls as part of your continuing education."

* * *

Agnes threw the bolt on her apartment door and collapsed into her lounge chair. She lay back, biting her lower lip, motionless except for a deep tremor she couldn't quiet.

She's lucky I didn't sink my teeth into her arm. Would have if I could've kept it out of court.

Taking slow, ragged breaths, she pulled out the phone. It almost fell from her shaky fingers.

At least I kept her busy until the screen locked itself. Could've been worse. Could've been a lot worse.

4-Brian Again

Moe arched under Cindy's palm. He stretched extravagantly across the worn laminate table and rubbed his cheek against her knuckles.

That drew a smile from Brian. "You're the only person that damned cat lets near him..." He cleared his throat. "Krysta worked my nerves, and we had differences over how the institute treated the kids—differences that weren't improving with time—but I wouldn't wish harm to her. So what is it I didn't know about?"

"She's dead, Brian." There was some complicated shading in Cindy's expression as she tucked aside an unruly wisp of snow-dampened hair curling free of her braid in the warmth.

A void opened up in Brian, and shut again fast. He spoke in a dampened voice from somewhere off to one side of himself. "An accident? The virus? She was careful, wouldn't ride with me until I showed her I'd had my shots. What happened?"

"Overdose—from the acting director's personal supply locker, the institute claims. The girl and I didn't part on good terms, and that's not sitting well with me." Cindy's complicated face made Brian think he wasn't far off target about what might have gone on between her and her painfully immature tenant, and that maybe her easy conscience didn't have as firm a footing on the dance floor as she liked to pretend.

Pursing her lips, Cindy jutted her chin toward him in a small nod that acknowledged what was running through his head. Then she moved on. "Trying to find my way past the official statements. I'm digging in places I'm not supposed to, so if I tell you anything I might learn, kindly keep it to yourself."

Brian nodded, his thoughts foundering with questions he couldn't articulate yet.

Pratt again. Nobody got into that medication locker but her. Carried the key on a lanyard around her neck. Doesn't make sense. She trusted the girl, but enough to give her access? And why, if she did?

Cindy stared into some dimension he couldn't see.

He directed the awkwardness toward a common enemy. "That place is gonna get shut down. Couldn't happen soon enough. God, first that kid with the seizure that shouldn't have happened, then poor Ro and Miles, killing themselves, just young kids. Ro wasn't an accident. She was too sharp for that."

[That's correct. And thank you]

"Then the Russian girl, that Sybille, with her bad pregnancy she never should've had, and now this..." He sighed jaggedly, unable to keep up the aggressive stance. "Should've tried harder on a lot of fronts, I guess."

"C'mon, Brian, we've talked this through before. What could you have done about any of it? There's more to learn about who the father of Sybille's baby was, I can tell you that. Seems they're saying she had an in-house boyfriend, but they're not naming him because he's underage. Not sure if I buy it. That sister of hers isn't going to go away quietly. Keep it under your hat, but I saw a lawsuit she got a disability rights group to file for her. Artemida isn't pulling her punches, and good for her. Could get interesting."

[Yes, these people and their names are important. Our names. I'm not emphasizing the fact just because we're autistics. I must be mistaken. The names of dead autistics are never important, only the names of those we have been a burden to.

Sybille, my precious girl, my love I was too young to recognize when I could hold you warm against me. My friend always.

Need to step back a moment here, in the interests of objectivity.]

Brian pressed his face into his hands, and his voice cracked. "Miles too. I hope to hell they dig into his fucking 'treatment protocols' that drove him to it. Smart kid, that he could find a way to get past the surveillance, but God, what a waste..." He sobbed softly. "And Ro. God. Poor Ro. Out there in the cold, alone..."

Cindy rubbed his shoulder. "I never met her in the flesh, but I feel like I knew her from the stories you used to tell. Was clear you loved her, and why. She went out there on her own terms, did Miss Rowena—you did everything you could for the girl, down to trying to adopt her."

"Lost damned cause right out of the gate." Brian waved his hand. "Didn't know what else to do. Stupid idea."

Cindy frowned at the attempted interruption. "What could you have done that would've made them give her back her speech tablet? If you'd swiped it and handed it to her, they would've just had you thrown out and grabbed it back. She was always going to run if she found a way. You loved that pepper in her spirit. Wasn't your fault. You need to let it go—"

[Okay, I do need to say here that CareWell kept the old hardline disapproval of any speech aids. Actual humans communicate with voice words, and the whole point of CareWell was to get its subjects to effectively mimic actual humans, however much it cost them in processing power. You'll expend a lot of energy to plead for food if you're hungry enough.]

Moe and Cindy turned abruptly to the back window of the trailer, down the narrow hall, with the same alert, querying look. The cat's clear blue irises became thin, bright rings around his widening pupils. Cindy's eyes focused on someplace deep in the woods outside. If she'd had pointed ears, they would have swiveled the way Moe's deaf ones did, pitched to a signal emitted from behind a veil Brian couldn't perceive.

He felt a prickle go up the back of his neck. "What's that, Cin? 'S going on?"

"You said you saw her, or something that looked like her? That hunting trip disaster last month? Was it before you got bit and then fell halfway down the mountain, or while you were laying there? Because anyone in as bad shape as you were could think they were seeing Jesus himself the way we found you."

Brian felt sick. "Before I fell. After the bite."

Taking hold of his left sleeve, Cindy pushed it back away from his wrist. "Could've been the sepsis talking. Let's see that chomp, speaking of which."

A neat set of punctures in the pattern of a large canine pair of jaws showed shiny pink against Brian's pale, sparse-haired forearm.

"Looks better'n when we found you." Cindy's soft chuckle had some shadows in it. "Puffed up like a mushroom and your teeth chattering from fever. What the hell made you decide to fuck with those mongrels anyway? You know they're too much dog to be afraid of humans, too much wolf to back down, and too much coyote to respect any damned thing. Either let them have the cursed deer or shoot the whole pack."

"Wouldn't do that. A shame though. Was a piebald. Beautiful animal."

"Yeah, we love the sharp-toothed beasts, don't we?" Cindy smiled, showing her own large, bright teeth, and eased the sleeve back down. "You're a good man, Brian. Hadn't told you before, you were in too bad shape...it won't make it right, but Morn found what was left of your kill and saved the head."

Brian gaped.

Chuckling, Cindy gave his hand a reassuring pat. "Nothing ugly. Mounted it up nice so you'd have something to show for all you went through. Rite of passage. It cost you, but it changed you too, seems like maybe. I'm hoping you're holding on okay without that therapy you were getting through work. Kinda seemed to be helping for a while, not that I'd trust any of it. Anyway, Morn smudged the mount after, and he has enough NDN in him to make the smoke worth something, thinking you might want to do some kind of honor for the animal to clear things out. Might not be a bad idea."

[NDN=Indian, BTW. Inside joke. There was a residential school on the Taconic Behavioral grounds, and there are a lot of them around our shared underlands. I've learned a little from them. They can be funny as hell, right in the midst of it.]

Brian nodded and was quiet for a while, then rubbed his face. "Maybe you're right. Starting to register things in a different way since I came back, not convinced it's such a great thing though."

"Sounds like you're thinking of something specific?"

"Seen her since the mountain. Sure it was Ro, had the mottled skin, pale eyes full of anger. *Her* eyes, not a shifter pretending to be her, the way she looked at me. Was when I was driving the Pettiman girl home the last time. Tried to keep going, but that damned black coywolf with the limp crossed the road down at the bottom just after the turn. Had to stop. You know, when I try to remember what happened, all I can picture is that lame black one. No way its range went that far to be the same animal that bit me."

He stared out the window, re-finding his thought. "Anyway, was like she caught up and climbed in. Krysta felt her, could see it on her face. Scared shitless. I got worried Ro'd do something to make me wreck, sooner or later. Final straw on going back to that hell-pit. Ro had the kind of rage in her at the end that could keep a spirit nailed fast to an ugly place."

Cindy stood. "Don't forget to lock the shop up. I left the blower on the mat inside the door—big chunk of ice wants to drop out once it warms up. But let Morn come over with the plow until that back of yours eases up, okay? Promise?"

Brian gathered the coffee mugs. "Thanks for not telling me I'm crazy to my face, Cindy."

"Nope. I'm not the one who's going to say it, to your face or otherwise. Don't let that be one of your worries. Lot of gates to the world, and sometimes things come through them when the gears turn a certain way."

* * *

The same field, the same damned field. His old mongrel retriever support dog and the approaching storm. This time the black dog becoming leaner, taller, running with a lame stride. Getting closer. The ground, breathing...

Cindy's voice. "Morn's been trying to reach you."

Slapping around for his phone in thick darkness, Brian finally touched it. The screen glowed in response, with no alert about a call. Cindy had cleaned it up for him, blocking any CareWell numbers. She'd cut off an automated connection to some kind of behind the scenes app. It tracked his location, he was pretty sure of it, and whatever else it sifted out of his communications. He was glad it was gone anyway. It wasn't any call from the waking world that had pulled him out of his dream.

Moe sat at the foot of the bed, his eyes giving off a low shine from the screen light, and jumped down when Brian reached for a reassuring snuggle.

"Fuck you then. Next time, I'm getting another dog."

Moe stared like he'd heard and understood what Brian had just said, and didn't think much of it. He started in with his loud, moaning meows that had got him his name, yelling like only someone who didn't hear their own voice could stand.

Brian rubbed his buzzcut head. "Okay. What? Not going to feed you at this hour. Asshole."

Moe exited the room with an insulted flourish of his tail, the long, white plume just visible in the gloom at the doorway.

Trying to ignore the cat's noise, now coming from the kitchen, Brian stared in the direction of the ceiling. The texture of the acoustic tile got clearer as his eyes came more awake in the near-pitch black. He resisted the urge to scream uselessly at the animal, and then suppressed a more violent impulse to go shut him up directly.

He's been a friend to you, soldier, even if he is an asshole. We don't take things out on our buddies.

Then everything went silent.

Something had made the cat stop in mid yowl, and when it did, Brian didn't find it a relief. He held his breath, listening.

Every tree branch that ever rubbed against the aluminum cladding on the sides of the trailer seemed to be at it again. Brian tried to think when he'd last cut them back, but the sound hadn't been there a moment ago.

He slapped his hand on the floor to summon Moe, who could feel the impact through his feet and usually responded.

Nothing.

Taking his rifle from the bedside, he crept toward the bedroom door, wondering if he should turn on the light, or whether it might be smarter not to alert whatever it was screeching that he was up.

A low growl came from near the back window of the cramped living room, and Brian tiptoed toward the sound, his rifle ready. Moe was on the sill, fur puffed out, watching something. Brian stifled a small scream of laughter at the same time he felt an ice-cold wave wash through him.

The garden hose, the fricking goddamn garden hose, emptied for the year and disconnected from the winterized faucet, was dancing out there in the dimness. Dancing right outside the window. Running its fitting along the cladding ridges like a flirtatious stripper.

Dropping to his knees with the rifle beside him, Brian gave in to half-throttled hysteria. "God, we're all mad here, right, cat?"

The wave came again, this time roaring. He felt like his heart could freeze in the depths of it.

Rowena stood in front of him, holding her toy pony, pulling at the tiny stub of a horn on its forehead. The last time he'd seen it was on the mountain, its pale blue palomino markings illegible under the filth of the grave. Back when the coyote bit him and he was falling into sepsis delirium. Something about making him choose between the toy and Moe, and he'd chosen to save his cat from the animal's jaws. Devil of a beast, making him leave that piece of Ro behind to be torn apart in sport.

It was clean now, and Rowena tapped her fingers along it as if it were a communication device. Brian forced himself to look at her.

She was lovely in her way, appearing to be a few years older than the nine she'd been when she died. Now, she looked like an early adolescent, but her whole body was fretted with frost crystals. Brian half-expected her breath to come as a glittering fog, but she didn't breathe.

She approached him, and he looked down at the ordinariness of his swollen knees in threadbare flannel lounge pants.

A searing cold touched his forehead and he shuddered, realizing her frigid lips had kissed him there. He tried to raise his eyes, but couldn't bring them all the way to her face.

The toy spoke. "I'm sorry I messed you up. I thought you were strong enough to help me. It wasn't your fault."

The wail of agony held back ever since he'd gotten word that the child had been found dead forced its way out. "What can I do, Ro? How...with you like this? What do you need?"

There was no response.

When he could force himself to lift his gaze, he was looking at a late-middle-aged woman with kind, playful, light blue eyes and silver hair. Her aging skin was mottled with vitiligo.

Her fingers mimed using a communication tablet, and her synthesized voice was musical, with an undertone of utter emptiness. "Attend to the signs, sweetheart. I love you."

* * *

[And I do.]

Second Quatrain
5-Artemida

Artemida stumbled up the slick steps to her second-floor duplex apartment just as the sun broke over Lake Champlain. Her high-heeled boots didn't offer the best traction on the eighth of an inch of ice covering the splintering wood she'd forgotten to salt before she'd left...how many hours ago? The storm had come and gone, blown south by an arctic wind, chilling from wet to dry snow as it went. It was a good wind, her friend. Courteous to make sure she'd come home in a clear morning with a shining crust over the ground that contained the sloppy mess underneath until it hardened. The extra punch of cold the weather system brought with it refreshed her foggy brain.

The fucking lock was frozen again. She fumbled to get the de-icer nozzle thingy into the key slot.

Pretty buzzed. Yes. I. Am. Righteously. This big, pale-assed Russian slut has done well for herself tonight. In many ways. Burlington is perhaps not so boring as I feared it might be.

She threw her coat on the chair, stripped the boots off her puffy, aching feet, and lurched to the bathroom. Opening the medicine cabinet, she debated whether to take something to help her sleep through the day or just resign herself to a white night and slug down a couple caffeine pills to kill the headache brewing in her temples.

Opting for the latter, she tossed her head back and swallowed. Catching her reflection in the cabinet door, she noticed how much her eye makeup had smeared. It wasn't a bad look, actually. She pinched a strand of her crow-black bangs and wondered if she should give herself a red streak there. Or a blue one. Purple? No, silver-white. Definitely. Older and mysterious.

Yes. Settled. Now let us properly inspect what the night has gifted.

Dropping her blouse to the floor, she reached into her bra for the tiny packet.

Ketamine. For real. Pure as the Virgin Mother, uncut as a Frenchman. Didn't stare at it for long. Never let them see how hungry you are, right, Sybille? Because he wanted to watch me dance all night, tall and juicy, ruthless like a panther. Fat, clumsy me who turns into someone else when we throw the K-switch. So I danced and let him think it was for him.

Hell, I would have let him fuck me any way he liked for the rest of that bag.

I saw you through the tear I cut in the world for you last night, my beautiful sister. Did you see me, sweet girl? I wore your brooch to keep you with me—

[I hear you, sister-friend. Guardian of my love, our Sybille. Can you hear me at all? You are far beyond my range. If you find her, summon me closer. I am at your service. Under the right circumstances, I can do shit.]

Stopping mid-thought, Artemida grabbed her blouse and felt for the jewelry. The catch on the cheap enamel rose had come loose, and the pin dangled from the fabric. Snatching it as it dropped to the floor, she pricked herself. She watched the bead of blood grow in the heel of her palm, and then jabbed the point into her flesh more forcefully several times.

Yes, I think I can do it now. I can feel it. You're here. Asking me. Surging.

[Where? Please, oh god, please, where?]

Artemida kissed the brooch and wrapped it in the fist of her unbloodied hand. She walked more steadily to the cramped bedroom, then blew across her red-blotched palm as if sending the scent toward a framed page from a fashion magazine on her night table, a glamour shot of a strangely lovely, very young woman with near-white hair and impossibly pale eyes.

Smell it, Sybille. Channel the power into me. Drink and fill me up.

Goosebumps lifted the fine black down on her forearms.

Yes! Stay with me! Guide me. Use me.

On the knotty pine nightstand, another picture lay flat and unframed, this one a small black and white headshot cut from a brochure. The caption read, *Assistant Director Dr. Agnes M. Pratt.*

Artemida swayed lightly on her bare feet, eyeing the photograph like a martial artist, and then struck, precisely impaling the subject's left eye, the pin's steel point driving firmly into the wood underneath.

* * *

[Very nicely done. I used to watch you and Sybille as you walked the grounds, both of you oblivious to the cold. I saw you pass her the communication tablet doubly forbidden with its Cyrillic characters none of the staff could decipher to spy on what you said to one another. You were beautiful as you are now, but then you were thin like her, with the same gestures, the same not-quite-there-ness. Together, you were like photographic negatives of each other, tall, long-haired, her white-blonde and you obsidian.

It's like the end of *Being John Malkovich*, when the Cusack character can see everything, but can't affect anything. I'm out of range of you. Come back to the grounds, even nearby, and I can talk to you. Just come close. I understand you never want to go through that gate again.]

* * *

Behind the wheel of her ancient rag-topped Jeep, Artemida sang/murmured along with a burned CD of Russian trance music. She could drive to CareWell in her sleep, she'd done it so many times. Something made her need to do it again, though her sister had been dead for months. Clearing the feelings a little. Respecting the grief.

Passing under the glassed-in walkway had become a motif in her dreams, always with her sister flitting through, just out of reach. Sybille had wanted that baby so badly, loved it even as it destroyed her fragile seventeen-year-old body, wracked by hell knew what that went along with her otherworldly autism presentation. Comorbidities, they were called. Fuck that goddamned father for damned sure, fucking up a mute teenager who needed a cane to walk any farther than across the room.

[Agreed. That's why I'm here.]

Fuck her stepmother too, for putting Sybille in that place. Fuck her for trying to have the only person who cared deported. Fuck her for the slaps that still stung, and the makeshift bedroom in the basement of a mansion that had nine of them.

Breathe. Watch the road. Nobody's talking to Russians anymore about deportations, but it wouldn't be good to cause an accident with illegal substances still in the bloodstream.

Just a few more miles down the highway to the storefront activist lawyer in Albany she'd shown Sybille's DNA test results from back when the sisters had been planning to sue for child support, thinking they could get by on that. Back when they still had hope.

Something made her flick the player off.

[Hello? Can you feel me?]

Artemida's lips silently formed the words, "Hear me, come to me, cross the divide..."

[I. Am. Right. Next. To. You. Damn it.]

Her hair stirred, perhaps in the scorching blast of the single working heater vent or the winter draft leaking in around the roof canvas. She brushed a strand out of her face, then slapped gently at something icy.

[Yes, that's my hand. More or less.]

The Jeep's tires crunched through the hard buildup of plowed snow on the shoulder and came to a stop. Breathing heavily, Artemida pressed her fist against her heart.

[Easy...easy... Didn't want to scare you.]

"Who are you? What do you want?"

[I could ask pretty much the same thing. We both love your sister. Maybe let me try a thought form?]

Long, pale, strong, black-nailed fingers shook on the steering wheel. Then Artemida threw her head back and wailed like an animal, ugly, congested tears streaming down her flushed face until they trickled cold along her neck.

Finally, her heaving sides calmed. "Thank you, thank you, whoever you are. Thank you."

***

[So now you understand me, Artemida. I will show you what you need to know. Watch for the signs.]

6-Cindy

The snow blew horizontal past the window of Cindy's wi-fi reception shack. Second only to watching the summer thunderstorms come in, it was her favorite part of having the little building on the pinnacle of the ridge, up there in the cold and quiet. She'd charge her phone, laptop, and extra power supply down in the farmhouse and then climb the rocky trail up a half-mile of switchbacks to get to the tiny cabin. Looking down past a few big evergreens, she could see the house tucked into the hillside a few hundred yards away. It was a bitch to get to her aerie, and she liked that.

Years before, when her hair was still fiery red, she'd built the single-room structure herself over the course of a couple seasons, hauling scrap lumber up on her back or in the two-wheeled barrow. Morn had never begrudged her the building materials or the time, and that made her look after him all the more tenderly. As she inspected her handiwork for needed repairs, she let herself reminisce.

First night I slept up here, expecting him to climb up after me with his desires. Just me and the stars, no roof yet. Realizing he wasn't coming, and not disappointed even a shade, knowing I'd found what I needed.

Wedged into the corner facing south-southwest, most days she could get enough bars to do data-intensive tasks. Krysta had asked several times whether the signal was strong enough to stream movies up there, insinuating some fun female bonding thing to do together. Cindy had put on a better lock and installed a couple cameras to ensure she wouldn't get surprised by Krysta waiting for her one day.

It had been hard not to snarl at the girl. She'd been a toothsome little piece for one thing, and the temptation had become annoying. Playing her favorite games with a naïve and painfully conventional person already living in her home wasn't a smart move, and that had turned out exactly the way she knew it would.

Now she saw the backdoor tracker she'd slipped in the CareWell system's highest-status controlling device through Brian's phone had picked up one activity incident. The tracker was just a few strings of code she'd bought on a dubious website. Mostly, it hadn't worked, but now it showed not only the record of an outgoing message, but it allowed her to access the content. The data must have been unencrypted.

The file was sent as an attachment, without accompanying text. Only a single photograph, taken in a place she knew intimately.

* * *

[I think I need to butt out of this part. I don't have enough distance to be objective, and that's the portfolio I've been handed. It gets crunchy from here.]

* * *

As she indulged herself in letting warm tap water run over her aching knuckles for a minute after washing up, Cindy thought of Brian Nichols chiding her for never wearing anything on her hands. He might have had a point, although she couldn't picture herself using those silly-looking gloves with the screen-conductive fingertips up there where the cold had really bitten into her.

She'd tried for more information about the message than the address it was sent to and the photograph. The recipient wasn't a corporate email account, just a short, cryptic jumble of letters and numbers coupled with a megaconglomerate server. After spending a half-hour in the fading light and deepening cold searching for any meaning behind the name, she gave up.

The hike back down the ridge hadn't been pleasant. When she got in, thinking she'd have a bowl of soup with Morn, she found a note saying he'd be spending the night in town. Their freeform arrangement cut both ways, even though she'd taken more advantage of it through the years, but right then it made the farmhouse seem empty as hell. It was probably for the best if that mood was on him. Morn had only ever been good and kind to her, but she knew there were other parts in there and she was grateful he took them elsewhere. At least he'd left the woodstove well-stoked, and the animals were already looked after.

After her solitary meal, Cindy took out the laptop and plugged it in. She'd saved internal and public CareWell documents over the last few months. It felt like a good moment to go through them.

As she started sorting, she alerted the way she had at Brian's. There was someone, or something, around—but this time very close. She sniffed the air. A bitter tang.

"Rowena, is that you? I know you some from Brian. Morn's been trying to run interference for you, but he says he can't reach near enough to communicate."

A spoon slid from the drainboard and clattered into the cast-iron sink.

"Oh, for fuck's sake. I can smell you and I can hear you fine without any damned poltergeist shit. Won't try to hurt you if you show yourself, I promise."

[Smell me. That's what she said. I don't know how I feel about that. Okay, yeah, I know, I said I'd quit interrupting.]

"You're safe. You've probably seen us down in the underlands of the institute, except we look like coyotes or wolves when we shift, so you might not recognize me. If you want to, have a seat."

The silver-haired woman with mottled skin and pale blue eyes appeared in the chair opposite Cindy at the kitchen table. She waved a translucent hand at the laptop screen and spoke in a mechanized voice without moving her lips. "You want some help with that?"

* * *

Cindy lifted her imaginary glass to toast Artemida Izgoya, the woman Rowena had directed her to. "That mask is gorgeous."

Artemida leaned back in her threadbare week-to-week rented room chair and raised a toast in return. "Masking is my specialty. I have many. I enjoy that it's been the protocol for everyone recently. This is by a small shop near here. They took the interior parts of a good respirator and clad it in the leather to my design. Not only does it present the way I intend, it will keep me safe from the virus when it once again surfaces. I work with the company on affectionate terms and let them use my patterns for others, or I couldn't afford such things."

"So, the footwear too?"

Stretching her black thigh-boots in front of her, crossed at the ankles, Artemida raised one heavy eyebrow flirtatiously. "Yes. Very good eyes. They are a bit tight now since I became more plump, but it shows the fineness of the material that they stretch to conform so nicely, don't you think? Do you like them?"

"Very much so." Cindy wasn't knocked off balance by the force Sybille Ranks' sister emanated, but she was pleasantly buffeted. She hadn't felt that kind of bracing storm from anyone in many, many moons.

"You have not said how you came to track me down, Mrs. McCoy. I am interested to meet with you because you seem to know much about my sister's passing, but I would like to understand more regarding whose corner you may be in. I do not stay in the town that harbors the CareWell Institute because it is difficult for me to keep a low profile. I try not to be so easy to find, so I go where I might blend in better. I thrive in the cold, so this place suits me."

Sweetie, ain't no place you're gonna blend in, but I get ya. South End Burlington probably offers better camouflage than Albany for someone who looks like the zaftig lovechild of Xena: Warrior Princess and Pinhead the Cenobite.

Stretching her own lanky legs so the thick treads of her Timberlands were only inches from Artemida's black lambskin-covered toes, Cindy steepled her fingertips. "Let's say that a mutual acquaintance suggested where I might find you."

Her hazel eyes hardening with the analysis, Artemida pulled her legs back and sat forward. "Was this person a friend of Sybille's, by chance?"

"A good friend."

"But very young?"

"Yes. Sometimes anyway."

"So, would a fellow longshanks care to join a girl for a refreshing stroll by the lake? Let us get the roses back in our cheeks, and see each other's faces. It feels somewhat close in here, and the furniture smells of other people."

Cindy felt her teeth flash behind her plain cloth mask before she could suppress the grin.

* * *

The two women stood on the overlook of Red Rocks Park, in fresh, ankle-deep powder. Neither shivered. Cindy smiled to herself, feeling something deeply familiar, like driving through your old hometown and recognizing a street you played in as a child.

Artemida, who wore more sensible footwear for the walk, had just confided that she'd spent her childhood in Murmansk, the largest city above the Arctic Circle, and that other than in missing that landscape, she had little love for her birth country. She scuffed an aimless pattern in the snow with her Doc Martens. "I miss birch forests and the smell of seawater and industry, but it serves. It's colder here with no ocean to temper the wind."

"I've never seen the ocean. I don't know if I want to. It seems so terrifyingly vast, from where I stand."

"Perhaps I will show it to you one day, but the Arctic Ocean is the best, the vastest in my heart, and the coldest. It will make you want to throw your head back and howl."

Cindy shuffled uncomfortably.

"Lucinda, Lucinda. Lovely on the tongue. Why do you let them put this bland nickname on you when your rightful one shimmers with moonglow and reflected firelight?" Artemida's leather mask hung from her neck, her iridescent, bruise-colored lipstick visible in the twilight.

"You were saying about blending in and low profiles..."

I hope you put that makeup on just for yourself, and not because you thought you'd be unmasking for me. You're infinitely more interesting if you did it for the mirror alone.

Artemida turned and smiled as if she'd looked inside Cindy's mind. "Thank you for telling me your real name. Witches and wolf-women must keep so much of their magic behind their many veils."

That sent a jolt through Cindy.

Artemida's teeth glinted. "Yes. I know what you are. Sybille could communicate with Rowena after she crossed. She showed her the underlands, and helped her understand how to move in them once they realized Sybille would be dying soon and joining her. Yet they lost one another when my Sybille passed, and Rowena is an unquiet in search of her."

Artemida turned so her face was fully in shadow with the city-illuminated glow behind her. "They're both trapped within a certain sort of commuter's radius of the Taconic Behavioral Health complex grounds for eternity. Before her pregnancy killed her, Sybille talked about lanky, long-muzzled wolves there. Wolves that could move through stone and earth and that only a few could perceive."

Cindy felt the snow stinging her face. "You know, I'm cold."

* * *

Artemida opened the door to her spartan bedroom. Beside Sybille's picture on the nightstand, wreathed in dark red silk poppies, a wooden box was opened to form an altar. A foot-tall white-robed skeleton wreathed with roses and holding a scythe had snuffed blue and black candles in front of it.

Cindy's nose watered a little from the chilly walk. She sniffled as quietly as she could. "Santa Muerte?"

Artemida's voice was muffled behind leather again. "Not Russian, you mean? One of the many beauties of La Santisima is that she doesn't hold your nationality against you. We all emigrate to her welcoming shores in the end."

Kneeling to reach under the bed, she pulled out a vinyl briefcase whose dark rainbow sheen was worn down to a muddy murk. "It's falling apart, but it was Sybille's. She loved it, and she didn't love many objects. I like to think she guides me to learn what the things I put into it mean. We were half-siblings. To hear our birth mother, our fathers came from different planets, but Mother was strange enough to forge a bridge between us that sparkles like foxfire and burning sulfur."

Artemida pushed the open case into Cindy's hands. "Take good care of these. There are people who don't like what I'm doing. I think they'll be safer with you if something happens."

Most of the documents were ones Cindy had seen in the lawsuit materials, but a few were new to her, and plastered with handwritten Cyrillic turquoise and lavender sticky notes.

That playful heavy eyebrow appeared again. "Unless you can read *russkiy yazyk*, we'll have to stay fairly closely in touch."

7-Artemida Again

As Artemida pulled into the public parking garage, she flinched at the canned voice telling her to pay in the lobby before exiting. She tapped her temple to get herself back to the here and now. Noticing the mousy French manicure on her fingertips as she took the ticket, she wondered if she'd given up too much of her power in order to gain entrance to her stepmother's world.

She'd been taken as part of the foreign adoption deal because Tonie Ranks wanted the pale girl who looked like some fey, delicate ice-world creature, and the orphanage wanted to be rid of her ill-tempered, drab older sister. Thus she'd entered the United States as an emancipated teenage au pair. Except that she hadn't been allowed to care for the sister she'd have given her life for. Tonie had turned Sybille over to CareWell when the child didn't live up to her behavioral expectations.

[This part makes me so angry I can't... I will say that if anyone tries to tell you that autistics don't feel other people's pain, please smash their face with a crowbar. For me. Please.]

For today, Artemida had plucked her eyebrows more aggressively; she'd lifted the obsidian from her hair, replacing it with a nondescript light brown close to her natural shade. She'd swept the result into a simple twist updo. Manic Panic Deadly Nightshade black was on the side of the tub back home, along with Virgin Snow for the streak she'd been wanting to put in.

She'd prowled the Burlington thrift stores for an appropriate designer look, including a masculine blouse, trim slate-gray pantsuit, and oxblood flats that minimized her height. She'd bought a mask that harmonized with the suit color. Even if there wasn't an official recommendation to wear them at the moment, she felt better behind one.

[You'll notice a motif in connection with Artemida. Masking. It's a term autistics use to describe what they need to do to "interface" with non-autistics. It's exhausting and soul-depleting. Yes, believe it or not, Artemida is an undiagnosed autistic, but she knows it. Once her sister was branded, she looked into what that meant and saw her own reflection. Bear in mind that drug use has begun to affect her, as it does with many of us who use, legally or otherwise, to try to regulate ourselves in a world meant for other people.

Neurodivergence runs in families, although Sybille got a double dose of the genetics from whoever her father was. I want to show you how different we can be from each other, and from the stereotype. You'll find a lot of us in the goth and punk communities.]

There wasn't anything to do about what she was driving, but she'd chosen an inexpensive garage well away from the law office. The walk would help clear her head.

A Range Rover like the one her stepmother drove was parked in a far corner, away from the elevators where it might be contaminated by some poor commuter's touch. If she didn't know better, she'd have sworn the behemoth that had deliberately taken up two spaces for itself was Tonie's. Tonie would never walk a half-dozen blocks just for a cheaper rate away from the high-end commercial district. Artemida took the space immediately beside it, making sure to be close enough that the door-swing from the larger vehicle would nudge hers.

She took a few breaths to compose herself. There was more of a soaring feeling in her head than she expected. She touched the serviceable flick-knife tucked behind her bra strap and then felt like a fool. Still, it wasn't a good sign for their joint lawsuit that she'd been summoned for an initial conference by a Monde, Ashton & Cooper junior paralegal who'd given her a time to be there without asking whether it was convenient.

Artemida had not been born to a stripper with a drug habit for nothing. Distrust was her default setting. She'd learned to hoard what she had. The precious bag was still half-full back at her apartment, but she'd carefully measured out a short line to sharpen her perceptions. It would be easy to take too much, to get pulled in too far.

MUCH too easy to lose the grip. Get dependent... Oh, fuck, I did do that second line before I left. Shit. I've been driving on a double. Well, not really a double. They were short, two of them more like one club dose. But still, the walk will be good.

Her shields were up. She hadn't shared any of her blackmail-quality information with her stepmother's attorney when he'd contacted her. It was troubling that he knew she might have something worth overcoming the animosity for. She hadn't even given copies of the documents to her own lawyer, a pro-bono activist who'd been working on pulling CareWell's operating license for more than a decade. She kept only the originals, passed those onto the woman Rowena had led to her, trusting that was the safest place.

Rowena had seemed an honest ghost.

Somehow the meeting had been scheduled for exactly the day her lawyer had an out-of-state court appearance, and the lawyer's junior partner who might have attended in her place was to take a deposition from a Taconic Behavioral Health maintenance worker at precisely the time specified by the Monde, Ashton office. The paralegal had been very specific about documents she was to bring. She didn't mention to the paralegal she'd left those documents with Cindy. She planned to just show up and let them all talk.

The little hairs along Artemida's back rose. This was a trap. She'd been an idiot to pull in next to that monstrous whale she couldn't see around. The old Jeep's engine wasn't shut off yet, and she depressed the clutch. The doors were locked, but the ragtop wasn't much protection from anything that meant serious harm. A stench of rubber smoke billowed when the tires squealed as she backed out of the space. Something dark loomed behind the clouded, weather-shredded plastic of the rear window, and then the Jeep impacted with a heavy thud.

There should have been some human sound, a scream of pain or yell of rage, but there was nothing. For an instant, Artemida considered opening the door to check what might be there, but then she engaged the four-wheel drive, pulled up so the front bumper hit the painted cinderblock wall, and then slammed into reverse again, riding up over a nameless thing on the pavement. She didn't look behind her, even when she fumbled with her cash in the garage lobby to buy an exit ticket.

* * *

The Nerve was empty in the early afternoon of a weekday. The club's sound system was lowered to a seductive whisper. If cops or ambulances were headed for the garage, Artemida could hear them. She'd turned off her phone before she left the Jeep at another garage even farther from downtown, and far away, too, from where she was now. This time, she wore a black hoodie pulled from the mess behind the seats. It hid her face but it was also warm, and she was bone-chilled, in disguise even from the self who was never cold. She was sure what had just happened was real, but her brain was trying to tell her she was imagining it. Self-protection. Trauma response, the therapists always said when her mind played now-you-see-it, now-you-don't. She wished she hadn't left the half-bag at home, but she was glad she had.

As she huddled and shivered into herself in a deep chair grouped with a circle of empty conversation seating near the door, a smooth contralto voice came from an open door to the service pantry. "Can I get you anything to ease the pain, sweetie? You look rough."

Barely raising her head, Artemida kept the hood low and pulled down her mask. "You probably could, but I'm trying to quit. This is the place that got me started, now I'm back, trying to look the Devil in the face. But yeah, I need coffee or something. Smells like a Starbucks in here. Thanks."

"Sure thing. I just put some on. Nice and fresh." The voice was connected to a tall, unmasked woman with cropped hair, much too elegant to be working behind the bar. There was something familiar about her.

Artemida mentioned that fact, continuing the conversation in spite of herself. Smalltalk wasn't generally her style. It was as if something was pulling her strings from far away.

"I'm one of the owners, but you can't tell anyone." The woman gave Artemida a confidential leer. "This place is held by a shell corporation. Looks better that way, right?" She loaded a tray with two coffee mugs and fixings. "Don't usually handle this side of the business, but staff has been evaporating lately. Drew the short straw since I'm off my real-world gig this week."

After setting the tray on the round glass table in the middle of the circle of retro-styled plush chairs, the woman parked in the one opposite Artemida, slid off her low-heeled pumps, and tucked her slim legs under herself. She didn't bother to adjust the leather skirt that rode up as she did. As Artemida leaned forward to take a mug, the woman smiled and reached over to slide the hood off her head.

"Oh my, such secrets you must have. I thought I recognized you. You used to be a skinny goth type, right? That Sybille Ranks' sister?"

The mug slipped in Artemida's hands. She managed to set it down with only a little slop. Her mouth moved slightly, but she didn't answer.

The woman kept her hand on Artemida's cheek, fingers sliding into her hair. "Or perhaps this is a temporary look? Your hair is brittle like you just pulled a lot of color out of it. Maybe? To even the playing field, I'm Kelli Rivers, assistant director at the CareWell Institute. Your sister was beautiful enough to be the model she was, even if it was a niche thing, and so are you, whatever this chameleon act is you're doing. I hope you did some photo shoots with her before she died. The two of you together were breathtaking."

Artemida's fingers trembled around the mug.

"I'm on your side, believe it or not." Kelli stretched her legs out and leaned forward. "I've been talking to the state inspectors. The rest of the high and mighty don't know it, but they're in for a surprise. That place needs to be cauterized. Agnes Pratt is a toxic human being and a vile clinician."

Artemida held the mug more firmly. "I'm listening."

"I think we might work together, do you think? I'm pretty sure you know things that could take the place down. Perhaps we should go in the back to discuss this. The evening crew isn't likely to get here early, but you never know."

With her lips clamped firmly, Artemida looked down and frowned.

"Maybe I should rephrase. I have something in the back you might like. It could help clarify what you want. You said you came to look the Devil in the face. This stuff will make you see angels. I did a couple of lines last night. Woke up feeling clean and sharp, no hangover. Would be nice to have some company today." Kelli stood, cupped Artemida's chin in her palm, and brushed her lips along the top of her head as she undid the clip on Artemida's French twist.

Glancing back across her shoulder, Kelli gave an appreciative nod as the hair tumbled down. "That's better. You look more like yourself."

Artemida's hungry gaze followed the leather skirt as it moved toward a doorway at the far corner of the sun-filled space decorated with monochrome lesbian photography. Finally, she lifted out of the chair as if drawn by a magnet.

It took a moment for her eyes to adjust to the windowless space. Kelli closed the door. There were faux-candle sconces that gave off just enough light to see. The room was for customers to indulge their private needs, and Artemida had been in it many times.

"I started without you." Kelli smiled. There was white powder on her upper lip. "Didn't know if you had cold feet." She gestured to a generous line laid out on the mini bar and handed Artemida a short disposable plastic straw.

Waving it away gently, she said, "Have my own, thanks. Don't like to waste any on a mustache." She pulled a three-inch brass tube with a drilled ball on the end from her pocket, set the ball in her nostril, and leaned over the line with her elbow on the glass, shoulder toward Kelli, letting her hair fall around her like a curtain. Then, with her hidden hand, she swept the line up fast and wiped it as far inside her hoodie as she could reach. She made an elaborate acoustic mimic of tapping the brass against the glass and snorting several times, and then she came up grinning.

Kelli giggled. "Wow. Greedy bitch. Looks like we've only got a few minutes to chat before you go catatonic."

Leaning into a corner for support, Artemida pasted a quizzical, woozy smile on her face. There was a lot of silence, as if Kelli was timing something out in her mind.

With a sharpness that made Artemida wonder if they were both faking, Kelli got to the point. "Tonie told me you didn't show. Even Pratt's finally on board. Makes it clean and easy now, since she's resigned herself to throwing Fallowfield's memory to the wolves. We're going to settle without you. Tonie says you're too stupid not to go along if she throws you some scraps, but I'm thinking she underestimated you. Our guy watched you leave your apartment, let himself in, found no documents. Then our other guy followed you to either escort you to the meeting or take them off you if you were recalcitrant, and now he doesn't answer his phone. Why is that, Artemida? Are you upset about something? I had a hunch you might turn up looking for a little balm for the soul." She started patting Artemida down, hands running down her sides, around her waist, and into her kangaroo pocket. "You got a folder stuffed in that jacket?"

"You are some kinda shit. Wow. N'wonder Syb hated yer guts."

Coming up empty, Kelli folded her arms. "Now, were you lying to that sad old lawyer about having the results of a prenatal paternity test for your sister?" Kelli was close enough that Artemida felt her heat. "I'll give you that Hamish was vain enough to send a spit sample to some shady-sounding foundation for the study of superior heredity that we can't track down. But if you don't have it, there's not much reason to keep you around. The board already approved the settlement and cut the check. They'll cut a fatter one if Tonie has proof of paternity. If you're not going to play along for a bigger score, then we don't want you here trying to get a piece of the one we have."

"Fuck you." The words slurred. Artemida used the wild surges of terror flooding through her to represent becoming incapacitated. Her head lolled and she slid a few inches down the wall. Her legs, though, were steel springs underneath the act.

Reaching for a thick throw pillow, Kelli said, "I think you can still hear me, right?"

Artemida dropped into a crouch, half-closing her eyes.

"Gel cushions are really soft, but they're not exactly, um, breathable. You are in the way of people who matter more than you do. Who do you think is going to bother looking deeper than the toxicology when I call you in to the friendly local cops and say I walked in and caught you hoovering up a line that would drop a horse?"

Making a humming noise, Artemida shook her head sloppily.

"Okay then. At least you'll go out happy." Kelli raised the pillow to place it, and then forced it down over Artemida's face.

Everything got very clear. Artemida's hands were steady. Blind, she reached into the sweaty space inside her shirt, flicked her knife open with one practiced snap, and surged up with all the power in her legs, her other hand guiding the blade to its target between the ribs up under Kelli's left breast.

* * *

The burner phone Artemida kept in her Jeep almost slid out of her hands a couple times. Since she didn't keep any numbers in it, she had to enter them on the keypad; it took a few tries.

Ro, please, girl, make this go through. Albany's a stretch for you, but please hear this. Make her pick up.

8-Cindy Again

Cindy looked away from the road for a moment to check on Artemida. She was curled against the passenger door, her bloodied hoodie wrapped around herself, the hood pulled mostly over her face. "Honey, we need to ditch that thing. Empty the pockets. I'm going to pull off at a road that leads to a dumping site a few miles from here, and we are going to chuck it down the hill, along with your contract phone, which I'm going to smash. This is not a request, this is a statement."

Artemida made a contrary, pleading whimper.

"No. You can borrow my jacket. I don't need it. It'll still be warm from me wearing it. I'm pulling off now."

* * *

The next evening, Cindy watched Morn come up to the farmhouse front door and then close it after him.

He said, "Okay, got the Jeep disposed of. Bené swapped a full set of papers for the chop. She's now Daria Esterhazy, Hungarian-Canadian French-speaking father, naturalized Finnish mother. Born in Saskatchewan, came here at fourteen. Start drilling it into her. Took the few things you said from her apartment, careful not to touch anything else. Was unlocked, ransacked, bedding and clothes slashed, so nobody's likely to notice a few bits of this and that. They may regret that bit of bullying. Used a burner to report it to the Burlington cops with pics as an anonymous worried friend. Crap photos, but good enough to show it was a shitstorm. She coming round yet?"

"A little." Cindy took her husband's coat and offered him coffee. "She let me cut her hair. She looks cute as a butch. Picked up a few pairs of jeans and some shirts for her at Vincent dePaul. Got a couple of sports bras at Walmart. She can wear our boots, tried them on already. She's a wreck though. The guy she hit in the garage died. It was in the news. Nothing yet about the woman at the club. She tried to help me out a bit in the barn, but she's walking around in a trance."

The steps upstairs creaked.

"Well, look who's coming down for supper." Morn waved Daria/Artemida to take a seat. "Ms. Daria Esterhazy, I trust you've come to enjoy my wife's cooking. I hope you were able to give her a hand with it today."

The newly minted Daria looked down as if she was waiting for Cindy to answer for her. When she didn't, Daria said softly, "Well, I tried to anyway. I'm not very good at it yet. Thank you again for your help and patience, but I'm very lost."

Cindy kissed the top of her head and set a steaming, delicious-smelling pot on the table. She turned to Morn. "I'm going to introduce her to Brian tomorrow. He's been needing more help lately, and I said I'd have the next kid who wanted to apprentice here give him a hand with a few things."

* * *

"Brian was getting ketamine therapy through a clinic that's part of the Taconic Behavioral system. They tried him on MDMA first, but it didn't take. He was too depressed. The K seemed to be helping, but when he quit CareWell, that got cut off. He's a good guy and I think you'll like him, but he is definitely PTSD with some deeper stuff going on." Cindy trod carefully along the icy ruts of Abenaki Ridge Road, occasionally putting her hand out to Daria so they could steady each other. "That's all I know about it. Morn just picked that bag up because he didn't think it'd look good for you if the cops found it there. We can dump it somewhere where it won't poison anything if you don't want it around."

Daria wiped her nose on the sleeve of one of Morn's old barn jackets. Horns stuck out of the top of her borrowed backpack, the mounted deer head giving her the look of having small, skeletal wings. "Do you think this Brian could use it? Please throw it away if he can't, but if it would do some good, yes, offer it to him."

* * *

When he answered the door, Brian looked down to watch Cindy kicking snow out of her boot treads, and then he seemed to register the large young woman with short, bleached hair standing next to her with his mounted buck head protruding from her backpack.

Cindy gave him a wry look. "Brian, this is Daria. She's, um, shall we say she was very close to Sybille, although I'm going to tell you to forget that about her if anyone should ask. I thought you might be able to tell her more about what happened. And yeah, we've all seen Rowena, so we can stop dancing around that. Nobody thinks anybody's crazy, okay?

* * *

Morn passed Cindy a strong, steaming cup of black tea and kissed the top of her head. "I like your friend."

Smiling, Cindy scryed into the dark liquid, looking past her reflection into the mystery. "That's a rare thing."

"Heh. Seems like Brian likes her as well. Would be nice if she'd help you as much. She's been down there just about every day, and doesn't seem to me like she's given you more than a few hours in the barn in the time she's been here. We can't rent out the room with her in it, she's got nothing left to her name, and she's not exactly working her way either."

"That's fine with me, Morningstar. I prefer my days quiet."

Morn warmed his crippled hand against his cup. "Why'd you agree to bring her back here with you? I know she's in trouble, but you've hardened your heart before. You don't usually like to bring them home."

"She needed me to. Not one I can go against so easily."

Morn chuckled low. "Now that's a first."

"Not like that. It was the spirit—the dead girl—that sent us to each other. Have the feeling if we don't keep faith with her, things could get ugly. Could get ugly anyway, a lot churning around in this, but we need our allies." Cindy frowned.

"Yep. Not trying to make light of it. This Daria pitches serious spells. Could feel them passing through on their way." He nodded at the memory.

"Did you figure out what she was casting? Lot of different languages going on. I got lost."

Morn shook his head.

Cindy reached for his good hand across the kitchen table. "You look like the arm's bothering you today."

He rubbed his wasted left bicep and down the forearm fretted with twisting scar tissue where the skin had been torn away by a piece of farm equipment. When he did, his clawed fingers jumped. "Yep. Storm's going to be worse than they say. Mark me."

"Good. That means we'll both just have to stay here and get to know each other again."

With a slow grin, Morn renewed the clasp and wagged their hands together. "Did I ever know you, woman? I'm not sure of that."

"Better than anyone else."

"Perhaps that's not saying much."

"Cuts both ways, mister."

* * *

The sleet seethed and slid down the windows ahead of the cold front, and then it froze, building up an impenetrable blur on the weather side of the farmhouse. The lee glass looked out onto the blank white of the hillside, a claustrophobic nothingness.

Cindy stared at her phone. There were no signal bars on it to be had anywhere in the house, and she wasn't about to climb the hill to her reception shed.

The girl is just going to have to hunker there with Brian, but I wish to hell she'd at least try to make contact. Maybe she's trying. Don't like this not knowing. The cell tower might work for a text even if it won't carry a call.

Cindy sniffed at the air. There was something in it she recognized, but it had never come up the ridge, even in the worst times. It was like the smell of desiccated fat on a mummified animal skin, not rotted or rancid, but overwhelmingly stale and utterly dead. The stench had always stayed in the underlands before, and she and Morn often had to guide captive spirits from sliding toward its cavernous well.

Morn paced, talking his callsign gibberish into the ham radio, getting responses from around the mountain coming in on the local repeater. He kept trying to reach Brian, but nothing came back. Someone identified only by a string of random letters and numbers said they'd take over the contact attempt. Morn thanked them and went out to the lean-to to refuel the generator.

When he came back in, Cindy brushed the ice from his dark, gray-streaked beard. "We need to go."

He nodded. "Yes, I think we do."

***

When they had tenants in the house, Morn and Cindy would keep their shifting process private, and they'd be forced into the attic. The leap from the roof had been exhilarating, but the convenience of setting up in the big parlor across from the kitchen outweighed it. Cindy half-hoped they'd jinx themselves and Daria would come straggling in to find them in mid-shift.

Morn brought in his smudging kit, the bundle of dried sage tucked under his damaged arm and the fragile symbol-painted pottery bowl cradled in his good hand. That was an aspect of the process Cindy hadn't used when she'd brought her own Celtic blood and Appalachian traditions into the marriage and its most sacred rite. Morn was a product of ancient lines, ancestors from the local Abenaki people, assimilated settlers, and escapees from several incarnations of the institute who'd taken refuge at the farm, going back to the Jogues residential school and the old state asylum.

The smudging made their motionless, vulnerable human bodies safer during the time-out-of-time that they were beyond them, and it purified the gateway they passed through so they wouldn't bring spiritual contaminants with them.

As her mate circled the long room, singing softly and wafting the pungent smoke with a fan made of a dried crow's wing wedged between his clawed fingers, cold drafts buffeted the soft haze into swirling currents. The low light was made stranger by the ice coating on the windows that cast oddly mottled shadows on the worn carpet and wide, bare floorboards. Cindy noticed a few pine needles from the now-gone Christmas tree that she'd missed in her sweeping. She put the housecleaning out of her thoughts, sat at the round card table, and lit her candle, safe in its heavy, silver-rimmed glass serving dish.

Morn smiled and sat down opposite her, his teeth long and bright in the flickering glow, like hers as she felt them grow in her mouth.

* * *

Despite the urgency of their foray, the pair roughhoused briefly in the snow, all snapping jaws and powerful muscles, tails puffed out in mock aggression, yet there were no prints on the white ground to mark their game. It was a part of their ritual, helping them shed human language and complete the move into their true forms. Their eyes shone, and their coats, one black with faint, finely speckled markings, and one a deep, auburn-tinged brown over gold, crackled with life. Then the stench wafted up, and they turned to their duties. Though the black one had a heavy limp, they covered the mile from the crest of the ridge down the spine in an instant, leaving no trail.

* * *

Flesh-world coyotes moved alongside the female shifter. She felt their interest. They shared thought forms with her, images made from scents and sounds, the vision inside a moving eye. The pack circled respectfully and let them pass, acknowledging their protectors and ceding the territory.

The shifters approached the human place. It was the kind one who denned there and their new apprentice who'd been helping him that the pair had come to check on. Something was not right. The reddish-furred one stopped, her hackles up, and the dark one sniffed the air, his ears slightly back.

A fierce scream came from behind the clear place in the wall, and the tiny white-furred protector hit the hard transparency between in and out with battering paws. Its hisses and cries were powerful, and the red shifter knew it was a potent being and a friend to their friend. She tried to approach, but the protector shrieked harder. The water tube below him outside flopped around like it was injured, and then something from the woods screamed hard enough to ripple the surface of being.

The flesh coyotes sprayed snow as they whirled and ran, and the distant screaming went on. The black shifter moved toward the sound in a gimping crouch, and the red one went to move by his side, guarding his weak shoulder.

The shriek threatened to rip the shifters apart. They could feel tears in their integrity, but they went forward. This was what they were created to do when their lives were formed, and they followed it, despite the pain. Finally the sound became so destructive that the black shifter sank panting into the snow, a thread of red trickling from his nose. The red shifter stood over him, between the force and his heart, and she screamed back even though her throat was made to sing and howl, the effort shredding her voice, but she fought to cancel the waves, fought until she, too, dropped to the snow, bleeding.

She had done her job. There was silence.

* * *

The candle had burned out. Clear daylight came in the windows, the ice sliding down the warming glass. Cindy let out a rasping sob and wiped blood from her lips. Her eyes focused, and she looked for Morn across from her as he always had been when she returned to the flesh world, but he wasn't there. She breathed in fire and knives to scream again, but she had no voice.

A squawk came from the dining room where the radio was set up. A string of callsign jargon, and then, "...Taconic Tri-State Local Repeater attempting to confirm we are broadcasting again. Please respond if you read..."

Cindy staggered to the radio and croaked Morn's callsign as best she could. "Read you. Urgent, two men down. Possible one woman. Abenaki Ridge. Going down there now..."

Volta: Third Quatrain
9-Agnes Final

[Hope you noticed I haven't injected myself much over the last few chapters. I've been busy. I'm still busy. Catch you down the line.]

* * *

Agnes was pleasantly immobile. She hadn't felt this relaxed in a long time. Her memory was a comfortable blur. There was something about a vagrant she'd seen walking on the grounds...shapeless, old clothes, lugging a trash bag... She'd complained. Probably nothing, security had said. Yes, that was no doubt correct. He hadn't been seen since... Since when? Never mind, too much work to think about it. Probably nothing....

* * *

This time, the awakening wasn't so pleasant. The straps of the adult papoose board had been set tight, probably tighter than the ones she'd wrapped...around...

Krysta! Krysta? But Krysta's... Say it, Aggie. Krysta's dead. We tricked her into taking a lethal dose of Midazolam and then wrapped her up so she'd stay quiet until she drifted off...but that was in the time-out room with the camera that Miles broke. Wretched child, but it worked out well... I'm not in a time-out room, am I? No. Where...?

Agnes tried to twist around to see where she was, but the restraint board was too well designed. She'd probably requisitioned this one herself, since she was still somewhere around CareWell, on the Taconic Behavioral grounds anyway. How did she know that? She must be remembering something. There was pain in her jaws. But no, that wouldn't explain....

Think! Clear the cobwebs. How do we get out of this? First thing— know what the circumstances are. Someone knows about Krysta. Copycat type. How did they know what I gave her? Toxicology report. Anyone in the profession could guess. Kelli? Definite possibility. Something about that, can't bring it up. Damn drug. Plays hell with short-term memory.

The smell though... Maybe the utility area that ran under a part of the building? Damp. Cold. Thick with mustiness, but so cold the smell was like a dormant bear deep into hibernation. Pitch black, too dark to see her breath, though it surely hung thick in the air, but yet her eyes seemed to supply information about the space around her. She knew that was a trick of her mind, but how would she know enough of where she was to provide the memory?

Study the illusion. What do we see? A flashlight glaring in my face, yes. Playing across...across acres of filthy old furniture, boxes, nameless piles of junk... Yes. Weird ornate fittings in spots. In the basement. Lot of money went into this in the day. Okay.

Cold.

Shivering powerfully against the restraint straps, Agnes registered the danger. This place wasn't heated. She'd been there for some time. Probably in warmer weather there would be the sound of dripping water. She wondered for a moment how she'd know that, but urgency cut off the rumination. It was cold enough for hypothermia to set in quickly.

The old state asylum buildings on the far side of the grounds. Used for storage.

Maybe the administration building. Was the fanciest one. I'm inside the granite foundation and it's winter.

The mottled girl...

[Hi there.]

***

The silver-haired woman stood above Agnes, illuminating the space with some kind of light source that appeared to be pure, glistening frost. "You may have to think a moment to figure out who I am, Dr. Pratt, but I'm the reason why you're here—not, you know, in the general sense—but the very particular, very chilly one you're trying to squirm your way out of at the moment."

It was impossible to perceive her clearly. Her lips didn't seem to move as she spoke, and her hands were making some kind of repetitive motion. Maybe a stim? Like the clients. Was this some kind of Autistic Liberation nonsense?

[Getting warmer. In one sense anyway.]

The shimmer coming from her fingers was so bright it left holes of absolute black when it left one spot and settled on another, like the negative sun that comes after staring at the real one. Probably an attempt at deception. Some trick designed to impress a vulnerable mind. Literal sleight of hand.

Agnes found her spirit. "No, I don't know who you are, but this could be construed as attempted murder. You'll be facing consequences."

"Oh, the rich, rich layers of irony in that response, Agnes dear. First hint: I'm dead, as you will be soon. If you follow the rules, the main part of your experience of eternity will be before your heart stops beating. If you fail to absorb your lessons, sadly for you, eternity will last long after your heart has turned again to the dust it always was."

I'm hallucinating. I'm sure of it. Pull yourself out of it, woman. Keep fighting. Keep warm.

"Well, yes and no as to the hallucinations. And yes, I can perceive your thoughts. I asked for that skill special for this occasion, and the old dealmaker agreed. The Devil—"

Hah!

"Oh, Agnes, I heard that, and no, you can't foist this off on being one of the tricks you think he pulls. He's nothing if not honest. Take that in any sense you want—anyway, the Prince of Darkness, for lack of a better name, does have title to the place I'm stuck in at the moment, but the landlord has humor and flexibility." The woman stooped, hands on her knees, to lean over Agnes. "Hint number two: you have a scar on your nose from a bite I gave you."

"Oh, nonsense! You must be at least fifty. That child was—"

"Nine. And at the moment, I'm performing, um, let's see..." The woman held out a hand, still dancing with words coming from her fingers. She examined it for a few seconds. "Yep. You're correct. Just about a half-century. At this point in the life I was never able to have, I've become a full professor of Disability Studies at Northwestern. Another decade and I'll make dean of the program. Buuut, of course, I'm dead, so much the loss."

"You? Foul-tempered little wretch. Hardly. More nonsense. All the more reason to ignore your Satan-spells." Agnes spit the words out through chattering teeth.

"And yet, you seem to be coming to accept that I am who I am. My name is Rowena, and if you take the first part of the premise, that this is the same foul-tempered little wretch who sank her very real teeth into your nose, then the second part becomes more difficult to evade."

"Go on back to your Devil then. I'll have no part of you. You always were a little fiend, and that seems not to change, whatever form you take." Agnes made a brave show of it, but she was aware that her shivering had lessened, and that this was not good.

[Welp. I tried. We shall do this the hard way.]

* * *

The vagabond again, with his little cube flashlight waving around, talking to empty space. Agnes was no longer shivering. Her body was cold and quiet, and she drifted in and out of consciousness. She vaguely remembered strange dreams where the vagabond was a woman full of cold light.

She sighed.

He looked at her. The face *was* feminine under the heavy brows and watch cap. The full lips moved, spewing warm clouds of breath and words. "Going for a wee ride now, Pratt. Every step is going to bump, and every bump is for my sister. For all the others who've died in the flesh or had their spirits killed by this place. You may consider yourself honored to be the latest sacrifice toward justice. You're going to be joining an old friend of yours."

That sounded nice, an old friend. There weren't many of those. "Lovely…"

[Nope. No joy from this one. She's still buzzed enough from the waters of Lethe and lack of blood to the brain that she's not likely to regret a damned thing. Sorry, boss.]

The vagabond attached the light to a strap around his head and picked up the restraint board by a makeshift handle at the foot. That wasn't supposed to be there, but it had made wrangling recalcitrant clients so much easier. She'd done a good job keeping the place going, short-staffed as it was. They'd all done their best…

The hiss of the drag across the floor. Choking dust. Then up. Her head hitting the steps through the padded board, again, again. Too many times, forever. Looking up at the ceiling of the stairwell, each flight more ornate as they rose. The vagabond stopping to rest on every landing, his heaving breath hovering in the brightness of his lamp. Then up. Bump, bump, bump.

* * *

The director's office glowed with faint, guttering gaslight. The hot, quiet clink and hiss of cast-iron radiators expanding with the pulse of steam through their veins. The rest of the building around and below an enigma. Beyond it, something impossibly vast and dark moaning and chanting to itself. The view through the high Victorian window dominating the space, utter blackness.

Hamish Fallowfield sat behind the massive desk. He was dressed as a gentleman of the late nineteenth century, on his desk a large computer screen displaying crudely made pornography depicting the unmistakably genuine anguish of barely adolescent girls. It was at an angle that could be seen clearly from the doorway. He made no attempt to hide it.

Rising from the leather chair, he greeted Agnes. "Welcome to Hell, my dear, or, I should say, a single quantum aspect of an infinity of Hells, all of which we must execute correctly if we have any hope of escaping any of them. In other words, hopeless, yet we continue. We may also choose the infinite mercy of the Abyss, if it will accept our gift." He waved toward the window, beyond which a booming howl began to resonate the glass.

10-Brian Final

The low, gray clouds had finally burst, draining themselves, flattening the tall grass. The lame black canine foundered, and Brian stared at it, unmoved as the animal sank into the stinking mud, thrashing. Clods of dark earth separated from the sod and collapsed into a sinkhole between them. The sinkhole grew, and Brian was unmoved by that as well, even though the edge drew ever closer to his feet.

* * *

"Okay, soldier, do you want to tell me about this OD, or do I need to send a blood sample down to the sheriff's office for analysis?"

Brian blinked at the VA doctor standing over his hospital bed. "No idea..."

"Deliberate or accidental?"

A few details fluttered through Brian's mind. He didn't want to think about any of them. He did grasp that if he admitted a suicide attempt, he'd be put on heavy restrictions. "Remember some dosage instructions, dunno if I paid attention."

"Instructions from whom? Not your regular counselor. I checked. You've been out of therapy for months."

"Nope. She was trying to help."

"She?"

"Said all I'm gonna."

"Well, you might be interested to know that your neighbor nearly died trying to help you. Morningstar McCoy's wife found him on your doorstep, collapsed. You're not the only one who's going to pay for whatever happened."

"Fuck. Said all I'm gonna."

* * *

Cindy sat stiffly in the visitor's chair, pushed in the corner away from the bed, her lanky legs pulled back so her heels were jammed underneath. "I let them in with my key, Brian. I'm no fan of cops, but sometimes they're a necessary evil. Would have been worse if they'd broken in on a search warrant authority. Daria's nowhere to be found. We have things to discuss later, in a more private setting. By the way, Moe finally let me get him in the carrier, and he's staying in the tenant apartment, if you care."

Brian felt another part of himself slam back into place, and he let out a groan of pain. "God, Cindy, yes, I care. Don't want to, but it's not working anymore."

"Morn had a fucking left-hemisphere stroke, Brian! His *right side*! Do you get what that means? I can't run that farm by myself! It's been in his family for a couple of centuries, and now I'm looking at having to sell. Finding a nice little apartment in town isn't that far from my idea of Hell. That's only the beginning of it, but we'll hold that conversation another time."

* * *

It took a minute for the panic to subside as Brian woke up, realized that Moe wasn't there, and then remembered why. The schedule he'd had to keep to care for the cat had slipped away, and bright mornings dissolved into fading twilight without any real markers to show what had happened to the time. The trailer was empty of every trace of him but shed tufts of white fur. The food, dishes, scratching post, and toys had gone with him. He hoped the cat was keeping Cindy good company anyway.

Scratching at his arm, Brian remembered more about his fall from grace, and tried not to push it out of his mind this time. The itch of the healing bite had become infuriating over the last...what, few days, maybe? The McCoys made their own herbal salves that worked better than the drugstore kinds that came in plastic tubes. He wondered if he might still have one of the jars of mysterious gunk under the sink somewhere. Or maybe the itch was telling him it was time to face the music.

* * *

Cindy set the bowl of chevre stew in front of Brian and turned away quickly. He heard what could have been a faint sob. "Yeah, I could use some help around here if you care to."

She cleared her throat. "Sold off about half the livestock, and working my way through butchering the ones too decrepit to market. Got any room in your freezer? Mine's full. Hate to waste good meat, even if it's not the best. Tough and stringy, but clean. Have to give what I can't put up to the coyotes, and they'd better enjoy it 'cause there won't be any more coming."

The savory smell fought with the anorexia of guilt. "How's Morn doing, Cindy? Don't blame him if he doesn't want to see me, but I owe him to at least pay my respects if he'll have it."

"Well, he's eating his dinner through a tube in his nose down at Albany Medical, and I don't think he's able to give a fuck whether you're standing there next to him or not."

"He was always so healthy, fit, good diet... Is that making any difference?"

With a hard sigh, Cindy sat across from Brian. He was relieved to see she'd taken a generous helping of her own cooking. "Yes, I think it is. Maybe, or at least I hope—"

A pleading yowl came from upstairs.

A faint smile broke out on Cindy's face. "Eat up, and then go visit your beast. Not sure if it's you he's smelling and crying for or the food, but the stew's been simmering since this morning and he didn't yell for it before. I'd appreciate it if you'd get your shit together enough to take him back home soon. I like having him around, but I need one more thing to take care of like I need a hole in the head."

* * *

As Cindy was showing him her evening routine, Brian looked down into the pen where the huge old black sow lay, gazing through the boards with a resigned expression. He turned to Cindy. "You're not going to butcher this one, are you? Thought she was kind of a pet."

Cindy suddenly bit her hand and turned her face to a support post, her back heaving with silent sobs.

While he waited for the storm to pass, Brian studied the pig's intelligent expression. She seemed to study him back.

No way in hell I could do this. Hunting is one thing, but raising animals under a death sentence is something else.

Wiping her tear-blotched face on her sleeve, Cindy sniffled and mumbled an apology. "Wouldn't be such a great welcome home for Morn, I guess. His Vajravarahi. Once a hippie, always a hippie with the weird names. Named her that when he bottle-raised her. The Diamond Sow Dakini. Can't think now how many litters she's had."

Brian looked away from the animal, unable to bear thinking of her having her children taken away to be eaten, year after year. His delicious dinner threatened to rise in his throat.

Cindy gave him a sharp look and wiped the last of her cry off her cheeks. "I don't have the strength to take care of the productive livestock by myself, Brian, and this one's past it. If you don't want to take her home in freezer packs, then you can come up and get her fed and cleaned up a couple times a day. For fuck's sake, you can't even look after your damned cat!"

Meeting the sow's eyes full-on, Brian said, "Welp, I guess I gotta get myself together. Said I'd help with the other chores. I'll do that, take Moe back, and I'd like to do my best for this old girl. Least I can to make all this a bit easier on Morn."

That's a fib. It's not for Morn, it's for the animal.

He resisted the inexplicable urge to bow to the pig as if she were some kind of divinity. She heaved herself to her feet, snorted, and shook the straw off her face.

He nodded to her and let out a sigh so deep it came from the ground under his boots.

* * *

Brian stood at the top of the gorge, the late autumn leaves underfoot brittle and dusty from drought. Twilight cast the lower depths in heavy shadow; he could just make out the sound of the trickling stream under thin ice. Behind him, the sound of the pack of mongrel coyotes, gorged but still fighting over scraps of the deer he'd shot. His lower left arm throbbed and swelled in his bloodied shirt, and he tore away his cuff to relieve it. He tottered, unsteady on his feet, his bad back spasming.

Rowena had been there, and he'd denied her. She'd crawled out from the buck's carcass, holding her stuffed pony. He hadn't fought for her. Hadn't challenged the black one with the limp when he tossed Moe in the air like a dog toy... Was that before or after he'd been bitten? After, after the poison of its jaws had entered his bloodstream. It was the sepsis, and it hadn't ever made sense, and never would.

Except that it painted a cruelly accurate picture. He'd wounded the buck with an ugly gut shot and had tracked it deep into a thin place, and things had happened, things drawn to feed on his guilt. He was a poison to the world, and he needed to leave it to heal without him. That girl Cindy had brought over had tried to help, had measured his doses and stayed with him through his trips, day after day, even offered her body to him, and all it had done was dig the hole deeper.

Couldn't remember much of the bite itself, only that the monster had confronted him over the deer. The animal had been canny enough to keep him from reaching for his rifle while the rest of the pack closed in. Whatever he'd told Cindy, he probably would have shot them all if he'd been able to get to his weapon.

Liar.

What good was any of it anyway?

He looked down, and then extended one foot out over the chasm. As he did, the plains of ruin that had been the country of his recurring dream rose up, their infinite horizons spreading, obliterating the forest where he'd just been. The damned black coywolf, injured on the far side of the growing pit at the center of the world, in danger of being swallowed. He reached out across the churning, widening void toward the flailing animal, but in trying to get to it, he slipped. He grabbed for the beast, slipped farther, and slid downward.

It sank its teeth into his arm, holding on as it dug its claws into the crumbling soil to drag him back from the foul, endless sinkhole. They both slid deeper.

11-Artemida/Daria Final

Daria's feet hurt. Back when she was someone else, they used to hurt from dancing in high heels, but those black lambskin lovelies had been shredded by a man working for her stepmother, and now she limped in heavy work boots that didn't fit right.

The hike back to the shelter was long, and the sidewalk had collected an inch of ice in places. Where it had been salted, the brine pooled and backed up, and when it leaked in around the stitching on her soles, it felt like fire on her blisters. Never mind. She had a bag full of first-choice, employee-discount donations from her gig at the thrift shop. Instead of three hours of minimum wage pay, she had the start of a new person to be. And she had fashionable boots that would fit, ready to admire on her feet once she got in, took a hot shower, and put on clean socks and fresh band-aids on her toes.

She rehearsed what she'd tell the in-house therapist about her choices. It was easier now that she'd come out as autistic in this newest version of herself; everyone expected her to be inarticulate and vague about her thoughts and feelings. That was the last thing she was, but she had a lot to hide, particularly now that she'd fully absorbed the fact that she enjoyed killing. Not indiscriminately. Not randomly at all. But certain people.

It had taken her a few days to get past the brain-jangle after she'd slid her knife into Dr. Kelli Rivers' heart, but then the memory just got sweeter every time she brought it up. She missed the spirit who'd first contacted her and gave her information about those certain people. Albany was a reach for a being bound to place. She was still hopeful Rowena might find her, so she'd leave a piece of candy or a cheap little unicorn necklace in hidden places as enticements.

That had helped her new identity, too, when the counselors would follow her and see some cute trinket tucked behind a curtain or on top of a plastic cabinet. They thought it was fey and sweet, and she played along, telling them her Finnish mother had always left gifts for the fairies.

If she played along well enough, soon she'd be able to afford a discount phone plan. The counselors would help with that. There was one who was quite helpful, and she rewarded him with a flash of her (old?) self sometimes, a sly smile with a curved hook at the end, a Slavic slanted-eyes flicker of playful wicked, but she was careful not to make it seem too assured, too familiar.

Any allies were to be treasured. It was still jumbled around in her memory how she'd made her way back to Albany, leaving the farm, leaving Cindy and Morn and their friend and his cat, just cutting out right before the storm hit, walking, waiting at the gas station ten miles down the road until she could hustle a ride. Old skills. Runaway skills. She'd never abandoned Sybille, but once Sybille was locked away, there was no reason to stay in that house. She got hauled back every time until she turned eighteen, but not because Tonie wanted her. It was just the law. And she ignored it. Rules were only as valid as the logic behind them, and there was no logic to making her stay under that roof.

Even as jailbait with mousy hair, thick eyebrows, and bitten-down fingernails, she could make men want to be with her and women consider possibilities. She put out if the exchange was worth it to her, and she made whoever she did it for feel like they'd been given something wild and powerful.

This new life at the shelter was just one more stop, and she'd started again from the very bottom to get there. Sometime soon, once she got her phone, she'd call Cindy, ask how everyone was doing, maybe visit again.

It was good back there with them on Abenaki Ridge, but she was in the way between Cindy and her husband, and there were strange things going on with that Brian that Rowena loved so much. It was like he let shit into the world that didn't belong there, and he was clueless about it, except that he wanted Ro to be alive again so bad, and maybe some of what he let in with her was a good thing. Unfortunately, not only Ro was using that entrance.

It wasn't as though he was some kind of warlock, he just left gates unlatched, and what came through them was a poison sometimes. It was still on her mind that she should have just thrown the rest of her baggie of white powder on the trash fire and stayed clear of the fumes until it burned out. Nagging thoughts about the stuff opening doors, and the man had doors opening around him all the time anyway without any help, and that maybe it might not have been the best combination. She'd tried, but the stuff he had going on was too much. Not even her tongue and the touch of her body could make that empty place in him heal over, even for a few warm, pulsing minutes. She regretted leaving him with that much of her old drug, but not because she wanted it back.

It had been time to get out. Right then, even with a big storm bearing down. Even with her few pictures of Sybille still in the bedroom she used at the farm. Even with boots that didn't fit, and a worn-thin coat that wasn't hers.

She'd said goodbye to Brian like it was any other day, and then she'd smelled something in the air and looked at the sky. Rowena hadn't answered when she reached out. It had felt like the spirit was stuck or fighting somewhere, maybe trying to protect Brian from something he shouldn't have let in. Time to go. Too many things left to do in places that weren't where she was.

Six hours huddled with an acne-scarred, thirtyish guy at a gas station with the power out. The storm swirled and howled around the building, bowing the big plate glass windows in and rocking the canopy, and she'd talked to the guy gently while he pretended not to be afraid. She'd lied to him in everything she'd said, given him the blowjob of his life, and then he'd driven her to the entrance of the Taconic Behavioral Health complex when the weather cleared. Then he'd picked her up a week later like she told him to, driven her to Albany, and when he did, she didn't tell him how to get in touch with her like she'd promised, but she gave him what he'd been waiting for.

* * *

The shelter counselor leaned forward and folded her hands on her desk. "Daria, how do you feel about your body? I know you've said that you do sex work sometimes, and you, at least on the surface, seem to remain unaffected by that, but I wonder..."

Hooo boy. Step carefully. She's working around to I Dent Titties.

"My body is something I put on. Meat suit. I like that term. I know, every therapist I've ever been to says I'm dissociative. Granted, I don't remember much from when I was little, don't know what's from being autistic and what's maybe from trauma, and if you know a single autistic who hasn't been traumatized, I'd like to meet them. Little hard to separate."

The therapist nodded sagely. "Yes..."

"Whatever, I'm fine with it. It's all performance and masks anyway, and it seems like most neurotypicals, if they ever see behind the costumes, they don't even see a human."

The counselor was one of those I-love-the-thrust-and-parry types. Not nearly as toxic as a behaviorist, but annoying. She did dress well though, and Daria's mind wandered to the cut of a blouse and the pattern of a scarf, picking up the string of words when half of it had already passed. "...can be about self-respect as well. What are your thoughts on that?"

"I do what I have to. What do *you* think about *that*?"

"I think you've been an adult when you should have still been a child, honestly. You don't need to be that tough all the time, you know. You're allowed to be vulnerable as well, and to love your body. Tell me, was there ever a moment you can think of where you felt good as a physical person?"

When I dressed hot and danced in clubs and got good drugs for it. When I dragged that pudgy bitch up four flights of stairs... Before that, when I held her by the hair and shoved some of her own nasty stash down her throat. Clamped her mouth shut for her. Didn't spill any and didn't get bit either. Made me think I'm still pretty strong, can still handle it...sitting, waiting in the ice cold, the same cold that was killing her, watching her eyes go out...

Careful, Daria Esterhazy. Your name is Daria Esterhazy.

Daria assembled herself into her best performance of a mental health professional's preconception of pedantic autistic presentation. "Not every culture carries the view that the body should be given such a high valuation within the full measure of the personality. Zen Buddhism, for instance..."

The counselor's eyes began to show signs that she was drifting, although she maintained her attentive posture with admirable self-discipline.

* * *

Checking her reflection in the common bathroom for the women's dorm, Daria didn't recognize herself for a moment. That wasn't unusual, particularly lately. The pounds had been falling off her with all the walking and the dreary shelter food. She'd let her eyebrows return to their former glory, keeping them tended and sleek but again formidable. One of her roommates, a beautician when she was sober, had tidied up the short boy-cut Cindy had given her into a respectable back-brushed pixie and added auburn lowlights.

As Daria looked more closely, a slow grin spread across her face. She had successfully absorbed something of Kelli Rivers into herself, and it shimmered around her like armor.

Vampaya! O yes, I can do this gig.

* * *

Daria jogged southward along the pond in Washington Park. It was a freakishly warm late-winter day, the kind that tempts buds to open too soon, only to be crushed by another hard frost. She smiled to herself, musing on who might be watching her and what they might think of what they saw. Only a gay man would be observant enough to note that her running outfit was from the previous year of the designer's sportswear collection, but she wasn't fishing for someone to go clubbing with. She had chosen the route through the park that would lead her near the law and medical schools.

She'd gotten a grant to take an online paralegal course, but she'd also been drafted by her favorite counselor to co-lead his drug recovery group, so passing between the twin educational monoliths was a fitting route. For now, she could take the course and make a little money too, but she'd need to come up with something soon. The shelter therapist was pushing her to make choices and move on. She'd burned a candle by her cot for Santa Muerte to help her decide which path to take, law or psychology. Each would get her into a different aspect of the world she wanted to enter. If she could do it under the protection of an admiring mentor, so much the better.

The Arctic Ocean had been in her dreams the night before, familiar and uncanny, welcoming and monstrously vast. Plates of ice heaved across it, fading into the frozen fog and night like a gigantic broken mirror reflecting the infinite void above. Somehow threatening and reassuring at once. A huge black mongrel wolf like the one Sybille had described, except much, much bigger, paced half-seen along the horizon, not sinking, not floating, but as if it had been born to walk on that churning surface, the turmoil supporting its paws like solid land.

Her dream swirled in her mind as she analyzed it for clues to her question, but then something brought her back sharply to the here and now. Ahead on the gently winding path was a sight that made her slow to a walk. A head of waist-length, graying auburn hair. Long legs with a powerful stride. Her stomach got a pleasant little rush of butterflies. Unlikely that it could be the one she thought of, but perhaps it was the sign she'd been praying for. Drawing a few paces closer, she matched her pace to her target. The resemblance, if it was only that, was even more striking.

The tall woman continued out of the park and down New Scotland Avenue. Perfect. The medical center would be on her right and the law school just past it on the left after the avenue curved west. Daria would get her omen.

The woman turned right, and went directly up to the Grecian portico of Albany Med, and Daria was sure of two things: she had her sign, and the woman was Cindy. She followed more closely. Cindy seemed to be walking a route she'd taken many times, not slowing in the lobby as she headed for the elevators. There was barely a flicker of hesitation as Daria followed, wondering when Cindy would recognize her. She stood a polite distance behind as Cindy summoned the elevator, and then got on after her and moved to the back corner so Cindy could have free access to the button console.

Apparently focused on where she was going, not noticing as Daria followed her off the elevator and down a corridor, Cindy passed a nurses' station and exchanged nods. She continued to a family waiting area. One of the nurses called after Daria in a mildly alarmed voice, and Cindy turned. When she saw Daria, her face made sudden, strange angles, and then she embraced her with a single soft sob.

Then she called back to the nurse, "It's okay. She's family."

12-Cindy Final

Daria had fallen asleep against Cindy's shoulder, sitting upright on the hard hospital sofa while holding her hand. The night nurse leaned into the room, fingers resting on the metal doorframe, silhouetted by the bright hall lights. "Mrs. McCoy, why don't you and...is it your niece? Why don't you let her drive you home and you can get some real sleep? We'll call you if anything changes, okay?"

* * *

Cindy had the wheel of the old truck; she wasn't giving up that much autonomy while she still could hold onto it. Daria worked her little burner phone, calling the people she'd been helped by through the shelter. The message was basically the same to roommates, counselors, volunteers, and the head therapist, but she'd given it personally to each one, the script apparently carefully rehearsed.

"Hey, I just ran into my auntie in town, and it turns out her husband had a major stroke. I'm going to be helping her out for a while. They have an old farm way out in the boonies, and she's going to need a lot of support to keep it going. I know it's a big change in plans, but we talked about me needing to find a direction for myself, and responsibility, and I think this is it. Don't worry, I'll keep up with my classes online. Gotta go, but need to tell you how grateful I am for everything. Okay, bye, I'm going to get choked up now if I keep talking. Bye. Love you."

Daria made nearly the identical call five times. The roommate was told she could have Daria's things, the counselor that she'd keep in touch, the therapist got added emphasis on her commitment to direction and responsibility, but otherwise the genuine-sounding speech, complete with tearing up at the end, could have been pre-recorded.

* * *

When Cindy went downstairs the next morning, Daria had breakfast started.

Outside, the creaks and clanks of farmwork starting for the day. A bruise-colored predawn glow etching the barnyard, dimly washing through the window over the sink. The little burner phone lying on the drainboard.

Cindy didn't say much, but she watched the young woman carefully.

Daria turned off the fire under the scrambled eggs and set a glass of cider and a mug of black coffee in front of her. "Um, I promised I'd keep up with those paralegal classes, but I'll need to borrow a laptop, and like you said, the reception in the house isn't reliable. Since you don't have satellite, can I maybe use your, um, your shed-house up on the hill to get a roaming connection? I can pay you back for whatever gets charged to your equipment."

Cindy was quiet for long enough that Daria started fidgeting, and then she put out her hand. "Okay. I'll trade you. You can have the key, but give me that phone."

A flash of something crossed Daria's face, but she handed the burner over and then reached up to open the cabinet for a plate.

Cindy stood. "Let me."

She let her fingers brush Daria's as she took out the stack of plates, set them on the table, and reached farther back into the cabinet. She took out a sleek, high-end cell phone. "Here, use this one." She held it so Daria couldn't see while she entered the access code. "It shuts down after fifteen minutes unused, so you better get moving. Do *not* lose it. It cost more than I like to think about these days. It's an onion—generates a new identity and location every time it's used. Untraceable."

Daria gave her a seductive grin.

Cindy patted her cheek. "Don't think I was born yesterday, lovely. I've lived in this house with a hunter and butcher of humans since before you were a babe in your birth mother's arms looking out a Murmansk apartment window at the tankers in the harbor."

"Morn...?"

"Yes, dear, and before you imagine you have anything on me in that game, see down there where Brian is?"

A stone retaining wall ran from the back of the house to the barn. Brian was sitting on it, and Vajravarahi rested her head in his lap, a dreamy expression on her face as he scratched her behind the ears.

Cindy lifted Daria's chin. "Could you go down there, right now, and slice that sow's throat?" She ran the forefinger of her other hand along Daria's neck.

Daria swallowed hard.

* * *

Cindy watched Daria scrambling up the hillside. Once she was satisfied she'd climbed far enough, she went to her real laptop, not the stripped down one in Daria's messenger bag, and brought up the security camera feed for the reception shed. She opened up a small window to keep track of activity on the eavesdropping devices she'd originally placed in the equipment to record her own use of it undetected. She also enabled the old stingray. It was an outdated system for intercepting signals, but if Daria had anything else on her, she'd at least know about it.

The exterior camera caught Daria as she let herself in. The interior one, a fisheye mounted in a rafter knothole, watched her wipe her feet and sit down where it could see most of what she did with her hands. She took out the phone Cindy had given her and scrolled down the few apps it had installed. The angle was good. Cindy zoomed in on Daria's upper body.

Daria entered a number on the phone keyboard quickly, as if from memory. The image of the phone screen came up on Cindy's laptop. The phone at the other end answered with an automated screening message.

After the prompt, Daria spoke. "Tonie, it's me. Your wicked stepchild. I'm sure you're disappointed to know I'm not dead. You might want to know what I—"

A woman's voice jumped in. "Artemida! Sweetie, where *are* you?!"

"Do you think I'd tell you that, after how your guy left my apartment?"

The voice at the other end hardly missed a beat. "He wasn't supposed to do that, honey. He was only supposed to be watching you—"

"To make sure I was going along with the plan while you set me up. I know that, and you might wonder how I do. By the way, my friend who went to check on me took pictures and sent them to the Burlington police, so you might want to keep some distance from that particular thug-for-hire. Too bad for you, he seemed like a loyal employee. Want to know what else I know? I know you were working with Rivers and Pratt to throw the lawsuit and settle privately, cutting me out. And see, now they're both dead. Along with someone who followed me into a parking garage. That's such a funny coincidence, don't you think, Tonie?"

"My god. You...did that to Rivers? And Agnes Pratt is dead?"

"Ooo... They haven't found her yet, I guess. When they do, they'll find Fallowfield too. That wasn't my work, it was a friend of mine. We have such similar interests, and we're still very close. The institute doesn't like the police looking too hard around the grounds, do they? Well, they'll find a lot, eventually, if anyone lets them."

Tonie Ranks seemed to gather herself. Her voice turned smooth and hard. "What do you want, Artemida?"

A voice like tungsten steel answered. "I want all of that settlement money, Antoinette. You hid it, so it's not like anyone will see you give it back. I'm going to text you a crypto wallet address that will only be active for a short period. If it is not in there within forty-eight hours, I will find you. If I learn you have held a dime back from me, I will find you. If you try to locate me, I will locate you first. Am I clear?"

"Will that buy you out of my life?"

"You can count on it."

"You have a deal."

Daria ended the call and keyed in another number.

Cindy's cell phone rang. "I thought I could probably reach you with this thing. Satisfied? That money should be enough to keep this farm running for a generation if I can get it out before the currency collapses. It should be about what I owe you, give or take a few hundred thousand. I'd suggest you find a good, discreet broker. I can recommend a couple if you want."

* * *

"It somewhat sucks that I'm never going to see the inside of the Nerve again." Cindy fed the woodstove and sighed. Afternoon light poured into the parlor, catching Morn's smudge bowl where it still sat on the big table.

Daria rested her hand on Cindy's shoulder as she stood back up. She guided a strand of long hair aside and kissed Cindy's neck. "I will try to make that up to you too."

* * *

Cindy's landline rang in the small hours. The two women had been sitting in the kitchen for most of the night. Even though the call had been on their minds the whole time, they both jumped when it came.

"Mrs. McCoy, I think you need to come in."

"Is it..."

"Yes, if you want to see him before we disconnect."

Cindy turned to Daria. "Can you drive?"

Resolve: Couplet

13-Rowena

Thin dawn trickles in through the heavy filth on the tall window with ornate moldings, brushing the room with faint strokes of detail. A rotted Persian carpet, brittle papers strewn around, with some more modern ones. A laptop with a lighter layer of dust, lying on top of a rusting file cabinet with decorative fittings. A desiccated male body and a fresher female one lying together behind a massive mahogany desk flecked with powdery mold.

Artemida/Daria was telling the truth when she said I killed him. I did it for Sybille. And for Miles and for me, but really, I only had the power in me because I was doing it for Sybille. I reached right through time and space to do it. They'll never figure out a cause of death, because what he went through happened in another dimension. Also, it's likely those bodies will be sitting there a while behind that desk, and it'll be hard to even know what Agnes died of. Nobody really wants to look into the workings of places like CareWell. It probably won't be until the Preservation Commission does a full evaluation for historical status for the old administration building that they'll finally know where Hamish Fallowfield ended up.

Except that's not really where he is.

* * *

A few weeks after I froze, I caught him in the room going through his trophy collection he had stashed there, and I took care of what had to be done. Sybille's precious, fragile body. What he did to it gave me the rage I needed. Then I gave him to her. She was still on your side of the veil then, but she was so transparent, she carried a thin place with her, and she could move with me. I showed her the underlands of the institute and I made a deal with the landlord that I could choose the ordeal of the rapist whose child she knew would kill her. She said she had hope to bring it to term, but she knew. Her body wasn't made for that, and it was going to be destroyed. She felt for that baby though. Felt for it in a way I could never match.

This is how she explained it back then, when she followed the path I'd shown her through the underlands and found the present I'd left for her in a cell formed from volcanic stone—

Sybille had reached into the opening in the rock bubble and pulled out her prize.

This is how it went: [*Come along, I have something to show you.*

A shriek tore the landscape, and Sybille dragged her prisoner through the rift that opened when she pulled him through. They were back in the Taconics, in late winter. Weak gray light trickled over a swampy meadow. At the edge were bare trees, and from one hung the frozen tatters of a body picked over by crows.

This is your new program, Hammy. Rowena designed it just for you, and she thought it was only right that I should explain it to you.

Your task is to complete this scenario so it can be found as you see it. No motion will be permitted that doesn't bring you closer to the completion of your assignment. It will take as long as required. You may approach the tree, fasten the rope, and finish the tableau. Attempting any other movement is futile. Time will freeze where it is, and you with it. You will become so familiar with the setting that you'll be able to perceive the sky stop turning when you fail. Once the initial act is done, you must maintain presence of mind within the disintegrating body in order for time to progress, up to the point you see here.

After that, who knows? We'd all love to move on.]

That was my gift to her. I bought it from the Devil by selling myself to him in an indenture. I get out of the underlands when I tell the story right. Only you will know that, and he will know because you do.

* * *

I expect you get the parallel, the endless, inescapable repetition, the reward only for perfect execution, the program literally the Individual Education Plan from Hell. I did torture him some with that idea while he was dying, kind of the way Daria did with Agnes. Those two really do deserve eternity together, and they'll get it.

I showed Agnes the tableau with Fallowfield hanging from the tree, and she screamed and ran to him and pulled him down, but his head came off in the process, and it upset his concentration. He was so close. Because the head had to be in the right place to make the tableau, he'll have to start all over again, and all she'll be able to do is watch.

* * *

The kicker is, Agnes was always afraid of losing her mind. I've made sure she won't, she'll have to be his attentive audience until he completes his task. If her mind wanders, he fails. It's just a few months' time to the rest of us, but they're both going to be Zen masters by the time they get out of this. That's mostly the point. That's why the Big Guy let me set it up that way.

***

Brian stares at his buck head that Morn mounted for him before he died. He keeps going over that dream where the lame black coyote bit him to keep him from sliding into the Abyss, but he still doesn't get it. I told him to watch for the signs, and he does try. Here's a hint: the Devil limps on a foreleg skinned when he escaped from a leghold trap. Trappers who go after coyotes usually just want the fur, so there's another hint for you right there, free of charge. Check the title page.

The doors and gates that Daria noticed were left open all around Brian are mostly closed now. I probably won't be using them much anymore pretty soon. The Abyssal Gate that opens into the underlands beneath the grounds of the Taconic Behavioral Health complex slithered up along Abenaki Ridge that one time because everything had gotten so permeable along there. It kinda followed Brian home, looking for dinner. The Big Guy had to deal with it, because that's the way the world works, at least this part of it anyway, but he wants us to move on.

It's easier now that he just has to manage the underlands, and not live in your shared meatspace anymore. Daria saw him in her dream right before she got back with Cindy, walking across the half-frozen ocean. That's more or less what he looks like down here now, and the Abyss doesn't try to get past him so much.

14-Rowena Again & Final

My friend Miles hung himself in the open roof trusses over the time-out rooms. He disabled the security camera for the room he used to climb into them from. Same room Agnes used to keep Krysta quiet until she died. Oscar Wilde said each man kills the thing he loves, and that's the kind of love you get when you're at the bottom of the food chain; the people who claim to love you are the same ones who can drive you to wish you were dead.

Autistics have in the neighborhood of a fourfold suicide rate compared to the rest of you, some say a lot more. On average, we die a couple decades before you do of any cause. But still, the rest of the world cares more about making us seem "normal" than about what would make our lives easier for us, not everyone else...

Okay, I'm done. The boss is growling that I'm going to lose my audience if I start preaching, and then I'll have to start over with the whole thing, like Fallowfield. Back to the story.

So, yeah. Krysta in the time-out room with no working camera, and Miles swinging in the heating system currents overhead. But did the state inspectors—

Okay already. But it does matter to the whole structure of the narrative that those in power have a vested interest in keeping institutions operational, because they prevent "chaos" (i.e. people like me) from running amok in the larger world. Kind of like the Abyssal Gate getting out, maybe?

[He says he'll grant me that one.]

Poor Krysta, whose guts I hated for making me move piles of pennies around and put them in plastic banks for a full adult workday in a forty-hour week when my hands wouldn't cooperate well enough for me to pick my own nose sometimes. I do not love hugs. They are not rewarding. I would prefer not to be touched and squealed at. Tickles set off my neuralgia, and high-pitched happy voices hurt my ears. I'm sick of gummy bears and I would like my stuffed unicorn-pony back, thank you, Krysta. Krysta, who did it for the paycheck and being able to say she worked so hard with the poor, defective children, but also wanted to play with killers.

***

If Krysta hadn't messed with Cindy, she probably wouldn't have absorbed the wicked it took to go snooping in the files that implicated Fallowfield, but once she got in, she didn't reckon on Agnes having teeth of her own. Kinda like Gene Hackman telling Dennis Farina to look at him in *Get Shorty*, acting as if she thought she was all that plus ranch on the side.

[Okay, sorry. Trying to be socially ingratiating with shared cultural references to engage the audience. Never was good about understanding what the rules are. Stick to the plot, right? You got it.]

I guess the last big thing to wind up is that now Daria has access to Agnes's spyware in the CareWell system. Also, she still has the paternity test results for Sybille, so if she comes out of hiding, as Artemida she has leverage. Nice way to hedge her bets. Maybe something to watch out for, considering that she's discovered how much she enjoys hunting. Always becoming someone else, receding until she emerges, teeth shining in the dark. I hope I'll be gone before she goes seriously searching for someone on this side of the veil to tell her about where Sybille is.

She and Cindy are doing pretty well. Cindy's showing her how to shift, and sometimes they still meet up with Morn in the liminal spaces. He likes that, and he's easier to deal with after they've been out together with the pack. The pack is always made up of killers. Hunters are killers. That's how they live. Daria fits in, Krysta didn't. I don't know where she is now, maybe because she doesn't seem to have grasped how you make the deals in this place. Morningstar is another name for Lucifer, if you didn't pick up on that already.

It *is* confusing sometimes. Having an interdimensional black hole roaring in your virtual, half-world ears all the time takes some adjustment. Morn always reminds me that it sings the song of mercy, so that no one has to go on if they truly don't want to. If they're dead enough inside, they can just stand at the edge, make eye contact, and let themselves get pulled in and it's all over. No memories, no pain. Nothing. Nothing, not even, so he says, any kind of blank-slate recombinant new life generated on the far side of being consumed. The Devil is known for lying, but if anyone knows the truth about it, it would be him.

[So I guess I do have to tell that part. Then I'll be done? This one's going to hurt.]

It's happening as I tell it as it happens, forever and ever until I get it right.

Sybille has been wandering around like a zombie carrying that rotting lump of tissue that would have been Fallowfield's child if it hadn't killed her. There's no light left in her beautiful pale eyes with the white eyelashes. Glorious freak. Too pure for *this* world, for damned sure. You shred my heart.

Anyway [deep frozen deadgirl breath] she just wanders over to the edge, and the Gate opens its maw for her. She stands there, holding that putrid thing that means more to her than all the lifetimes of love I feel for her, and then she's gone. There's maybe a tiny blip in the howl, barely registers if you're not listening for it hard.

She's gone. The one who did it to her is still serving his sentence. I guess maybe that's fair. It's his choice anyway.

Then the Big Bad Not-Even-a-Fullblooded-Wolf comes over and pulls me back. Actually, he has to sink his teeth in pretty deep to drag me away, because I'm just about ready to follow her in.

I flinch and then accept his offer, burrowing my speaking fingers that are a child's and an old woman's deep into his coarse black fur, and I hold handfuls of it tight while the great sucking wind tries to vacuum us down into itself, but the Devil's stronger than the Abyss, for here and this moment anyway, and I'm hanging on.

We limp far enough away from the Gate to be able to rest a bit, and then he tells me I'm free to go now.

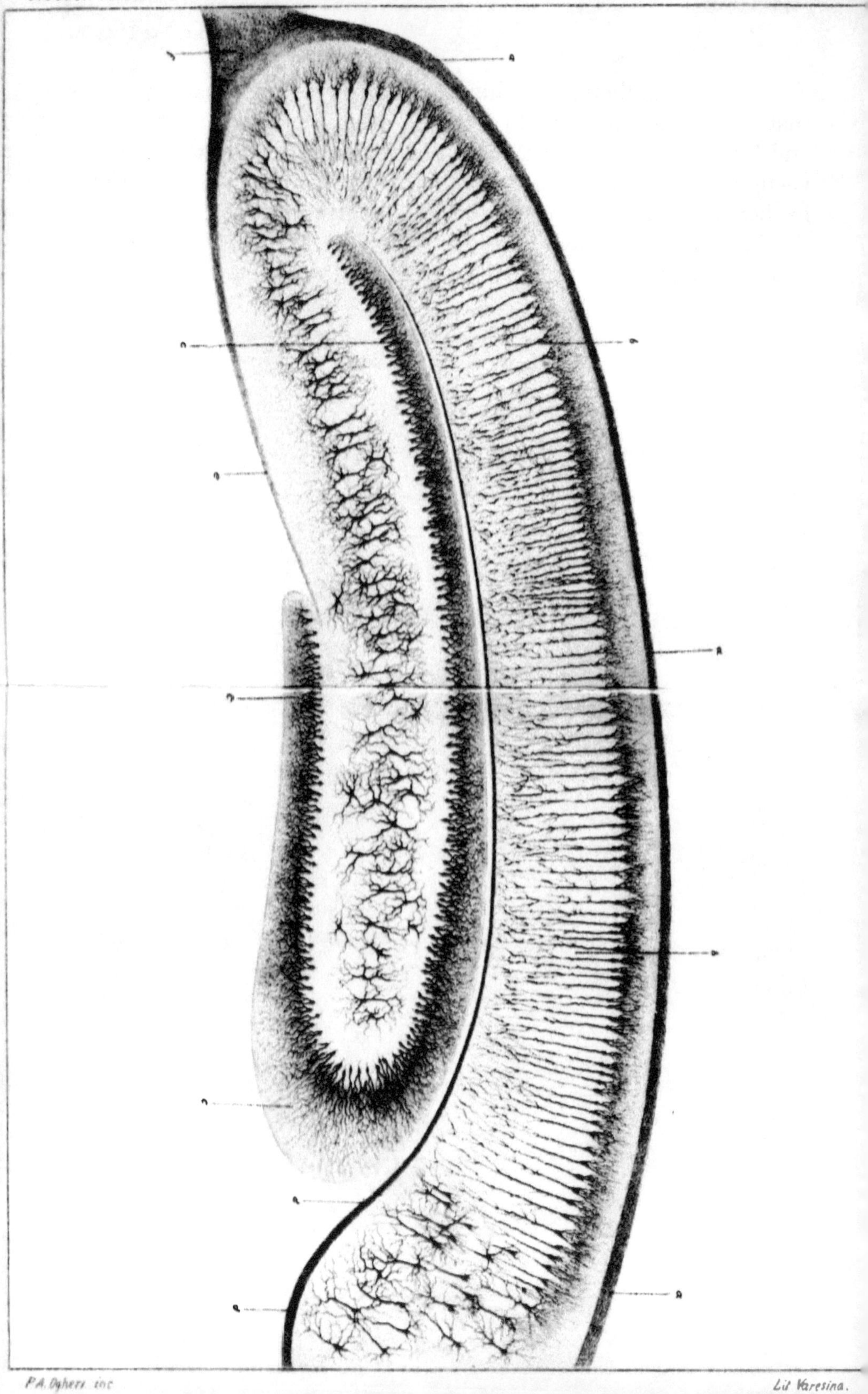

WHEN ALL THIS IS OVER

The worst thing would be the cat. Tiny, ancient, and post-traumatic, she's been attached to me like superglue from the moment I took her in as an emaciated, abandoned kitten a couple decades ago, when I thought my life would end much differently. I've tried to give her a feeling of safety, even if I didn't have it myself. Her medical bills are killing me. Writers don't bring in much, particularly not ones who work at the margins and don't have the stamina to adjunct teach anymore. I'd let her go, but she asked for help, crying like she did when I found her under my porch, her mother and the rest of the litter gone.

The slack vacancy I've received in response when I've tried to share Borges' *Aleph* have sapped me of the energy I might have had left to mask up and work behind a counter somewhere. Nothing is so deadening as a room full of sophomores disappointed at what they thought was going to be a sleeper class on Lovecraft—*Stories of Interdimensional Awe*—making clear they're terminally bored by a syllabus I've spent a lifetime preparing.

The college campus is closed now, and the library access that was my only worthwhile perk is cut off. I failed at developing a remote curriculum, and pleading an executive function disability only lost me access to health insurance. So now it's a flood-line tally up the walls of my life as to whether it's my medications or the cat's that submerges me deeper financially in a given month.

I've tried to do right by her. I didn't always get it—when she was tiny, I tried to scrub the irregular splotch of faint ginger tabby off her nose, thinking she was dirty. Schmutz became her name, even though she's always kept her tuxedoed coat immaculate, so meticulous she's let me bathe her occasionally since she's too stiff to groom herself as thoroughly as she once did.

Now that she's gone deaf, she's even more apprehensive. She

invariably hid from the visiting aides subcontracted grudgingly from the blue puzzle-piece charity. After being stung by bad publicity over their bookkeeping and tactics, the outfit did need to justify their tear-jerk fundraisers by showing they occasionally provided practical assistance to actual autistics, and briefly I had hope I might be able to stay afloat with that help. The "behavioral health" visits were subsidized, not gratis, and had as much unwelcome proselytizing as those where the evangelists live under another scripture, but they kept me from going under.

Even before the pandemic, the aides came only sporadically to scare the cat, help me balance my checkbook, make sure I'd paid my taxes and utilities, and check that my prescriptions were current. For a couple months, a nice one even brought me groceries sometimes, and didn't pocket the change until I told her she could. It was a lovely, ephemeral moment. The company that employed them still sends bills, but the visits stopped completely months ago.

A charity for the physically disabled drops off a box of dry goods every now and then, and I'm grateful for that, but it's not enough, and it only drags out the inevitable. I don't blame the low-wage, exhausted, and poorly equipped workers for not finding me and my executive function failures worth the risks, and I haven't filed a complaint, but it's made my choices harder and more limited.

* * *

Rowena looks down at her frozen body, her ethereal face hidden by shifting waves of golden and spun-glass hair, even as in her material death, it lies in a dull, grayish mat. My treasured character, my mottled (mobled?) queen waits in her default position, observing herself dead at the age of nine. Her immortal element is able to move freely in any direction to further the narrative. She's perhaps the most powerful player in this world-game I've created, and I haven't begun to do her justice. Justice was the force that forged her, and it no longer carries the urgency it once seemed to. At least the social-contract cards have been laid on the table face up now. We know where we stand. Pretending is too exhausting for any of us to maintain anymore.

I try to reach her, but her eyes only flutter briefly before returning to herself.

* * *

My youngish distant-cousin-once-removed calls occasionally, saying, "I'll come visit when all this is over." As my closest living relative, she knows she'll inherit everything I have left unless there's a will she hasn't seen. There isn't. She wants to see what there is to pick over when I'm gone; I'm not so obtuse as to human motivations that I've failed to work that one out, even though I barely know her. If she hadn't sent me photographs of some old family documents to introduce herself, I'd tend to think she was some grifting stranger who appeared at a convenient time. Unfortunately, she's blood. Relativity is a heavy, plodding old theory in which mass warps space. In my family structure, greed has generally filled in for mass in creating the gravitational funnel.

I've sold most of the good old books. I'm left with a few treasured paperbacks, including a 1955 *Lolita* that might still be worth something, but I'm not breaking up my Nabokov; I have every English-language softcover first release, a collection started by my father, and it will be someone else's job to dismember it. Nobody wants the silver anymore, not enough to pay anything for it. I'm considering setting everything on fire before I leave, killing my few treasures cleanly rather than leaving them to the vultures. I do not love my landlord, and the occupied houses are far enough apart to avoid risking others. In this neighborhood, the borough usually lets them burn. Herd immunity—the farther apart the inhabited dwellings, the less likely lives will be lost.

I'm taking too long to remove myself, at least the relative and I are agreed on that point, even if it's unspoken. I'd avoid her saccharine, hard-to-follow calls full of neurotypical nuance and doubletalk completely, but I don't want to risk a welfare check by some social worker who'll try to 302 me for involuntary commitment "for my own safety" because she can't be bothered to figure out what neurodivergent competence might look like, or an ill-tempered cop who'll tase me because I look at him in autistic.

Sacrifice the Weak, says the proudly displayed sign of a protester demanding the right to inflict her lethal germs on people like me. It's probably a matter of time. I dream constantly about being infected when I have to go out. The few friends who might have helped are gone or too vulnerable themselves to ask.

I made a choice, in this version of me, to devote myself to the life of the brain, not the heart. Those with my neurology rarely succeed at both, and I'm no exception.

In another life, instead of a couple of academic degrees, I might have had someone to be an ally, to support and be supported by. To cook for, and sew a button back on a favorite, neatly folded shirt for unasked, who'd help frighten away the vultures and jackals. Someone to share my home, other than my tiny, loyal little pale orange ball-and-chain who hobbles slowly after me, each of us taking one step at a time, up the interminably painful stairs to bed, her white-mittened paws brittle as dried twigs.

Another life, but not this one.

* * *

Rowena finally hears me, turning her head so the albino blaze of vitiligo down the middle of her face shows. Her delicate hands, raggedly marked as if she'd dipped them in splashing milk, turn to gnarled claws. She's aging as I watch, turning from a young woman to a crone with a shrewd, skeptical expression and clear blue eyes flecked with ice.

* * *

Antiques have lost value in recent years. The past as commodity isn't what it used to be. I sold the Peter Heylyn *Cosmographie* (MDCLII) and raised enough to pay the cat's and my medications for a few months. At one time it would have brought the price of a better home than the one I live in now, but I hung on too long. My parents were old when I was still in college, and I'm an only child of only children. The cast-off shells of their extinguished lives were all I had by the time I turned 40. I'm the tip of a fractal of human reproduction; my decomposing duplex where rats own the other unit is filled with a depleting pool of inherited books describing the glories of Western expansion and the inherent rights of superior races.

My form of autism is genetic, and strongly associated with the familial presence of schizophrenia, bipolarity, and similar neurological presentations that involve unusual patterns of brain connections. Most branches of my family tree have exhibited signs of mental variance. The majority of us have had good enough poker faces to avoid institutionalization, although keeping up the pretense, learned at our elders' knees, has been too exhausting in the long run. Survival has turned us into the feral brutes of the Next Frontier, subject to the civilizing discipline of behaviorists, our brains uncharted territory ripe for exploration by neurologists armed with magnetic resonance scanners and diagnostic questionnaires.

I ended up with these centuries-old volumes because my line died out, in good part because of its inability to navigate the modern world, disappearing into the grimy attic trunk of moth-eaten stereotypes together with the noble savage, humble peasant, and faithful servant on whose backs the pissed-away family fortune was built. My last few ancestors shuffled through cluttered corridors of once-fine houses, surrounded by echoes, isolated by eccentricities that would now be labeled under the guidance of the DSM-5 manual of psychological conditions.

I was born the year Sputnik was launched. Behaviorist Ole Ivar Lovaas was developing his techniques for torturing children. It was his mission to convert sexually or socially divergent ones into compliant case studies "indistinguishable from their peers." His work would become an ever-expanding, multibillion dollar industry. In a *Psychology Today* interview in 1974, the year I entered college masquerading as an academically gifted human being, Lovaas said of my true peers, "You see, you start pretty much from scratch when you work with an autistic child. You have a person in the physical sense—they have hair, a nose and a mouth—but they are not people in the psychological sense. One way to look at the job of helping autistic kids is to see it as a matter of constructing a person. You have the raw materials, but you have to build the person."

* * *

Rowena has moved into the Panopticon of the juvenile in-patient services building of the Taconic Behavioral Health complex. The complex is my version of *The Shining's* Overlook Hotel, malevolence in itself—and the Panopticon is its lucid-dreaming mind. Each screen shows the feed from a camera peering down from the ceiling, intruding its gaze into a child's dormitory, a classroom, lavatory, or one of the punishment suites where a strap-fitted platform occupies the center like the satin-pillowed four-poster in a perverse version of a master bedchamber.

My Rowena has temporarily merged into the collective, a swarm of spirits connected to that sinister locus, chained by the horrors in its history of socially approved cruelty. The site has been used as a residential school for Indigenous children and as an asylum which once incarcerated several hundred inconveniently outspoken women.

Like the most powerful chess piece, Rowena can move on any axis. She plays in four dimensions, not bound to the empire of the dead, whose citizens have been too stunned by the atrocities they've experienced to move on. She shares in their awareness, and makes her decisions after consulting with them, but is able to travel more immersively in time and space, her mind humming like a spider on its own string-theoretical silk. She ages and becomes a child again, and then necrotic as it serves her. She never speaks like a typical human though. Her voice is synthesized, as it was when her autistic fingers flew across her communication device in life.

The Panopticon is what I originally named the banks of surveillance monitors used in the all-too-real Judge Rotenberg Center of Canton, Massachusetts. Despite being legally and publicly challenged for decades, including by no less than Juan Mendez, the United Nations Special Rapporteur on Torture, the JRC continues its aversive-based behavioral conditioning as envisioned by Lovaas, defined by its signature device, the "graduated electronic decelerator," or GED, a remote-controlled electric shock delivery system strapped to the bodies of children under its control.

The spotlight that the UN rapporteur is putting on the school is given added poignancy by the fact that Mendez was himself subjected to torture by electric shock at the hands of the Buenos Aires police in 1975.

He was abused with electric prods.

"I feel very strongly that electricity applied to a person's body creates a very extreme form of pain. There [are] a lot of lingering consequences including mental illness that can be devastating," Mendez said.

— The Guardian, 6/12/12

The JRC meticulously chronicles its abuses, except when it doesn't. The Panopticon has been known to go blind at certain times. It did record the seven hours of torture of eighteen-year-old black autistic "student" Andre McCollins in 2002, strapped face down and shocked until he developed burns deep enough to require hospital care, for the nominal crime of refusing to remove his coat. His unwritten sin was being a young post-adolescent autistic of color who tried to reserve for himself a shred of dignity and autonomy.

A decade passed before the McCollins case reached the courts, where it was settled in private without limiting the JRC's right to use the devices. The FDA has now banned the use of the GED there, but as it's always been when activists have thought they'd won the war, there's no evidence that the ruling has been followed. There will no doubt be more battles to fight, and what the panopticon sees may be adjusted to protect the institution.

The meatspace JRC, designed by its behaviorist founder Matthew Israel, a true believer in the "transformative potential" of inflicted pain, has an arcade of storefronts and amusement games where inmates are allowed to redeem good-behavior tokens. The arcade is based on the *Wizard of Oz*, with looming animatronic figures of the Wicked Witch, et al. My version is built on Lewis Carroll's *Alice* books, and Rowena is a child-pawn becoming a queen in her own right at the end of the Looking-Glass chessboard.

Rowena is always at the end of the chessboard. She owns it outright, in fee simple. She reviews the monitors and extends her chequered net across the web of stories trapped on each screen.

* * *

My family has excelled at masking for generations. So long as we weren't in your presence too long and were otherwise in good form, we could usually fool you into thinking we were natively charming, smart, and capable—just like you.

The first sign there was something off about me was a peculiarity about my left eye. The pupil has always been larger and less reactive to light than my more ordinary one. I sometimes go red/green colorblind in it, so that when I close my right lid, the world is a dull wash of faint blues and pale yellows. When it's acting up, others notice the pupil spasmodically widening and contracting. For all that, I'm left-eye dominant, so old-style viewfinders always required me to jam the camera body onto my face, mashing my nose. My odd eye is my mind's eye, where the information wants to come in.

As I grew, my toenails were blue and my lower legs blotched purple when I wasn't lying down; pressure on them left oyster-colored marks. My ears roared and I felt faint when I stood up. My body was so out of synch with itself, and my mind so ignorant of my physical processes, that my chest expanded when I exhaled if I became aware of breathing, the emptiness in my lungs pulling a vacuum, and the air hitting a leaden wall of inertia when I struggled to inhale again. My joints flexed backward. I was branded a lazy malingerer for not wanting to participate in physical activities my uncoordinated body hadn't developed enough to navigate. Team sports were an onion-layered nightmare from all the aspects of my compound disability. I didn't learn how to throw from the proper foot until I was near fifty, only a few years before arthritis would claim my right hip, the joint ground down to bone on bone from a lifetime of misuse and doctors ignoring my attempts to explain something was deeply off in my biomechanics.

As it was, my lax-muscled clumsiness was only recognized as a cause for teasing, not one of the many physical signs of the genetic cluster of comorbids that ride alongside autism on the DNA ladder. Had I had physical therapy instead of the nightmares of gym class, I might still be able to walk without two canes, and I might have other options. I can't think about that though, because unlike the stories I create, this meatspace narrative has only one ending.

If given the choice of having the right physical care if I were being screened for autism as a child today, I still would rather go undiagnosed. I'm grateful to have avoided the intimately personalized torments of applied behavior analysis that would entrap me now. I'd have never made it past the dragnet of testing that trawls through the modern elementary school system, funded by the ouroboros of behaviorism.

Millions of dollars get donated every year to the most vocal of autism charities, and almost none of it reaches people like me. What help I get now comes from my physical disability, although my foundering mind is so much more wounded by the world.

* * *

...

* * *

I can't remember when I last slept, or if I'm sleeping now. I snapped the cat's neck—swung her frail body sharp and quick by her head—watched the betrayed light leave her eyes as she sighed the deepest final exhale of her life, over at last...only to find her huddled against me, gently snoring.

* * *

I had been to the vet, waiting in the car for them to bring Schmutz's meds out. The idea of having her euthanized was roiling in my head. I couldn't keep paying a couple weeks' worth of groceries for one bottle of pills, and she was on four different ones. I pulled my scarf down to breathe better. Even though it was cold, I needed the window open. I felt like I might vomit.

A person wearing a face mask leaned in. I thought it was the vet's assistant with the meds, but they were screaming in my face, screaming so loud I couldn't hear them. The mask had a Zumba studio logo on it, and berated me something about how I had more responsibility to others, because everyone else had to look out for people like me getting sick. I heard the words "fat," and "not an excuse," and "not even trying to do your part." A hand reached in to point at the handicapped parking placard hanging from my rearview mirror.

I couldn't form words to fight back. Then they pulled their mask down to scream at me better, and I realized she was shrieking at me for not having my face covered. That made me laugh. She was spewing scream-spittle into the car for me not wearing what she just pulled off. The laughter accelerated her into another dimension of explosion. She tried to open the door as I pushed her away to shut the window.

Someone yelled out from the vet's office. I drove away without the meds.

* * *

Schmutz is curled in my grandfather's rosewood cigar humidor. I would have sold it if the milk glass lining wasn't broken, but that means I still have it. It fits her perfectly. I laid her in it and arranged her one paw over her eyes and the other cupping her white bib the way she used to sleep, and she stiffened that way.

Don't worry, I was faithful to my promise to her to the end. She died peacefully in my lap while I was dozing. The deep sigh woke me. It was the most beautiful gift she could have given, and I'm more grateful than there are words for it. There was never a more loyal friend.

I'd thought to bury her under the peonies by the back porch

where I found her. I carried the box out, but couldn't find the place. The flowers were gone, and the ground was hard as cement. I remembered it was winter then.

* * *

Rowena is beside me in the car. She's telling me I need to pull over because I have a fever and I'll hurt someone if I get sloppy at the wheel.

* * *

We're by a lake. Not sure how we got here. It's big, and the ripples on it form strange moiré patterns. The shore on either side of us is dark woods looming above a low, stony cliff, with a narrow strip of pebbly beach. Rowena is wearing a small silver crown that's mostly just a glimmer in her windblown hair. She looks to be in her early twenties, and she's unbearably lovely sitting there on a rock outcropping, looking out over the oddly rhythmic water. Schmutz is rubbing against her leg, peach-orange fur sleek and shining in the low sun glaring across the interlacing waves.

Turning toward me, Rowena makes her fingers dance out the grace notes of her mechanically chiming voice. "You always were a good mother."

I smile. The heat of the evening sun makes my skin tighten.

Something occurs to me. "How did Schmutzie get out of the humidor?"

Rowena throws her head back, laughing. "Schrödinger lifted the lid. Just like you let me out of the isolation room. Her joker-self is still in there, so she's a cat without a grin. Where's your croquet mallet, since we're going by the book? Who let Jack out of the box? Kubrick never shows it."

I'm trying to think. In the stories, she's confined in a time-out room at night, and yet follows the villain through a passage that same night. I always left that question open, as a nod to Stanley Kubrick's version of *The Shining*. In the novel, the ghost is obvious and the boiler is the Angel of Fury. The mallet isn't in the movie at all, replaced by a frozen maze. Alice never got to hit the ball in Wonderland.

The light is scorching, so intense I can barely make out Rowena's form. It feels like standing in front of an open oven.

* * *

I'm shivering as I fill the gas tank. The plastic gloves that were in the dispenser by the pump smell like urine.

A large man swaggers toward me. "Take that goddamn mask off. You look like a Haji woman. Chicken-shit city car, I knew you'd be wearing a rag over your mouth before you even stepped out of that tin can. We live strong around here. Go on back to the chicken-shit coward city you come from."

He gets within inches of my eyes, still bellowing and waving his hands.

I jerk my mask down and hiss in his face. I can feel the noxious warmth of infection in my breath. His eyes widen as he backs away.

* * *

We're back at the lake, except I'm driving again, with Rowena in the seat next to me and Schmutz on her lap. The humidor is on the back seat. The car bumps across something...is it a field of wildflowers? The Emerald City glows on the horizon, and then sinks below it. The moiré lake has resolved itself into squares of black and white ice, glass windows and mirrors, extending to the skyline in every direction.

I hear in my head, "A frightful sphere, the center of which is everywhere, and the circumference nowhere."

The cracking sounds are loud as thunder. Deathlike cold begins to pool around my ankles.

Rowena smiles.

ACKNOWLEDGMENTS

Deepest thanks to the tattered remains of the East End Writers diaspora, in particular to Lucy Turner, who has gone well beyond duty in her skilled critique of the stories here. The work wouldn't be what it is without her investment of time and care, and I hope to partly repay the debt once I'm more free of the fog of my health wars. Also much gratitude to my dear friend Mike Scharf for his ongoing nurturing of my process; without his input I don't think these years of writing would be as true to our shared autistic experience as his tireless fellowship has made them.

Each of the publishers of the anthologies where some of these stories have appeared is owed thanks for their support, in particular C.M. Muller of Chthonic Matter, who offered early encouragement and an outlet for several of my more challenging pieces that I didn't think would be accepted into any good home. Thanks also to Jeffrey Thomas, whose supportive words have led me to follow my muse more trustingly when it comes to building the form and structure of my writing. I am hugely appreciative of Des Lewis for including a couple of the pieces here among his last Gestalt Real Time Reviews, in particular his wonderful insights into the final story of this collection. His ongoing interest in my output helps keep me trudging forward when I'm more inclined to set my artistic crutches aside and collapse into the recliner.

As always, it's a privilege to work with Scarlett R. Algee, whose light hand on the reins should never be confused with lassitude. A deft tug here and push there can make all the difference, and the skill is appreciated. Likewise, it's an honor to be on the JournalStone/Trepidatio roster for the second time.

And again and forever, thank you, Sue. None of this would be possible without you.

PUBLICATION HISTORY

Passed Pawn appeared in *Nightscript 6*

The Red King appeared in *Nightside Codex*

Extinguishing was originally accepted by Nightscape for *Weird Whispers*, then released from its contract when that project went on hiatus.

Polar Dawn appeared in *Graveyard Visits*

All other content is original to this work.

ABOUT THE AUTHOR

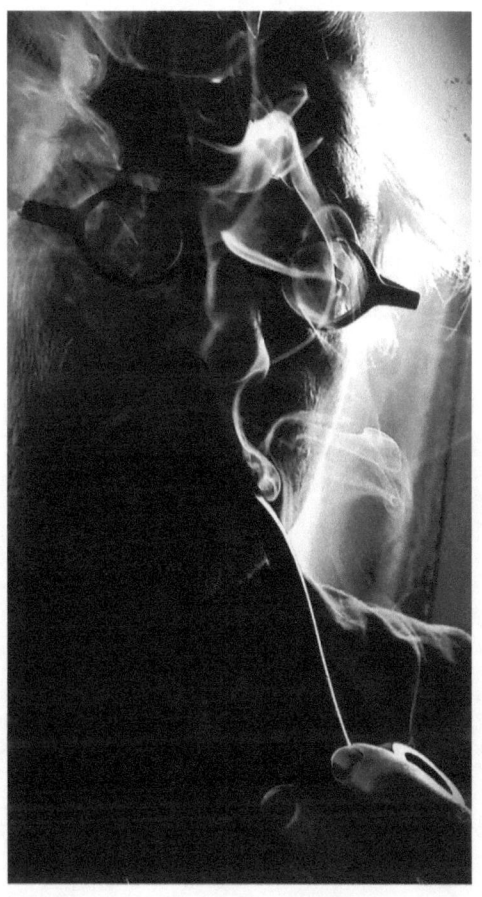

Selene dePackh is a queer, crippled, neurodivergent crone who spent most of her professional life as a graphic artist and trim carpenter. Her writing forefronts marginalized characters because she finds them more interesting. Kirkus describes her 2018 debut novel *Troubleshooting* as "a gripping, lyrical, and ambitious dystopian novel," whose MC is one of the "few protagonists in sci-fi—or literature in general—that present an autistic perspective with such specificity and pathos."

Her genre-fluid speculative fiction has recently appeared in *The Nightside Codex, Recognize Fascism, Nightscript,* and *Oculus Sinister,* nonfiction in *Slag Glass City, Heavy Feather Review* and the *Identities* issue of *Shooter.* Her horror novella *The Golden Road* was published by JournalStone in 2022.

www.ingramcontent.com/pod-product-compliance
Lightning Source LLC
Chambersburg PA
CBHW020654260626
47157CB00008B/3026